The C Dan Dames: The Lost Jewel

AKSEL K. TAYLAN

*To Tomer:
You can do anything you set your mind to. GL kid*

THE LOST JEWEL

Copyright © 2012 Aksel K. Taylan
All rights reserved.
ISBN: 1533375607
ISBN-13: 978-1533375605

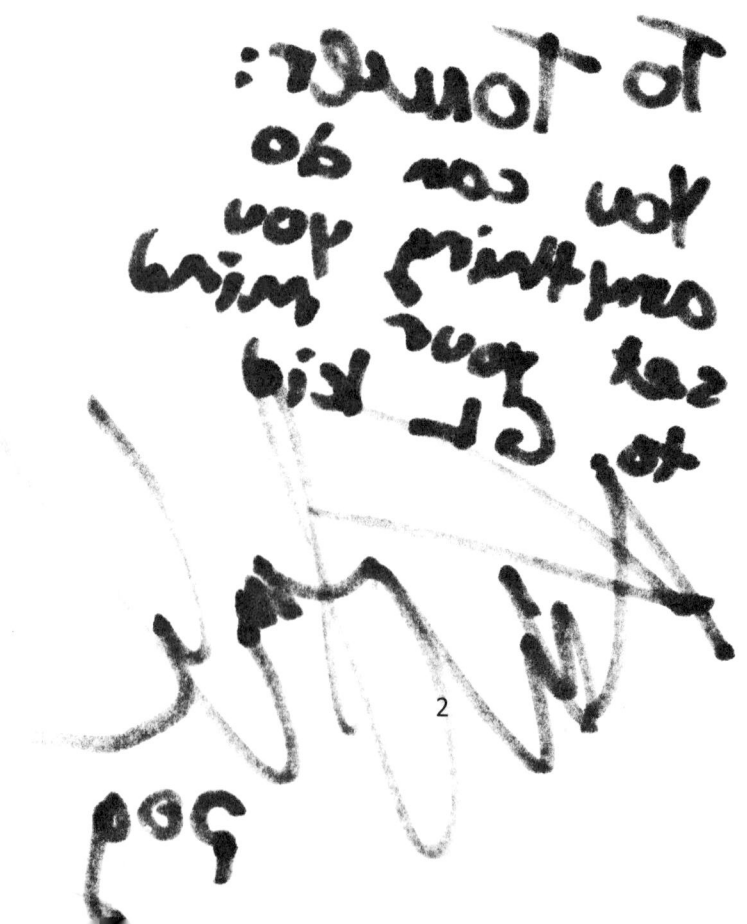

THE LOST JEWEL

DEDICATION

To my friends, who taught me to express myself and never be afraid to create.

THE LOST JEWEL

THE LOST JEWEL

CONTENTS

1. Finding the Way...9
2. Costly Fault...21
3. Behind The Scenes...41
4. Uncharted Territory...69
5. Stranded...95
6. Emergency Measures...108
7. Giving Insight...119
8. What The Ocean Holds...135
9. Native Traditions...158
10. Rescue In Progress...182
11. Time For Backup...196
12. Jungle Fever...209
13. Titans Clash, Only One Remains...214
14. Finale...220

THE LOST JEWEL

ACKNOWLEDGMENTS

Thank you to anyone who bought and enjoyed the first novel. Without you all, I wouldn't have been able to finish this one.

THE LOST JEWEL

THE LOST JEWEL

CHAPTER 1: Finding The Way

She was nowhere to be found.

This was all her fault. As these thoughts creeped into Vajra's mind, he could not escape the feeling that he would never see her again. He almost couldn't fathom the fact that his own daughter had caused all this. He watched as his beloved hometown continued to burn down to the ground. It was complete chaos; people screaming and running from their houses in fear of the eerie flames that spontaneously combusted the night before. Vajra shook his head again, a lone tear slowly making its way down his face. Suddenly, he was overcome with anger. This was not his fault! He repeatedly said this to himself, hoping it would make him feel better for what she had done. Unfortunately, there wasn't much Vajra could do but watch his whole life burn before his eyes.

She moved faster than she thought she was capable of, but still, she was not safe from the soldiers stomping behind her. She tried to pick up her pace, but this was as fast as she could possibly go and it just wasn't fast enough. In a split second she had an idea. She stopped and pulled the longest vine from a nearby tree, and tied it to another one on the opposite side. She carefully placed the vine on the ground and quickly hid it under some leaves and other foliage; camouflaging it. She did all of this in the blink of an eye and hid behind one of the big trees nearby in anticipation. Even if this gave her only a few minutes of extra time, it was all she needed to reach the hidden clearing that the soldiers would not be able to see from the path. Sure enough, the purple and green-suited men tripped over the vine that she pulled just in time, and piled up on each other. The girl made her escape. She couldn't help but crack a proud little smirk at her plan, but she didn't really have the time to enjoy the feeling.

Draped in a dirty brown toga with mud splattered all over the front, the girl was a mess. Her blue eyes looked grimy and misty. They had lost their brilliant spark to a dull distant gaze that hardly showed any emotion. Her light brown hair looked like an old broomstick, and her bare feet were crusted with blood and open sores from all of the running. Finally, she found a small space between some trees and bushes that seemed hidden from the path the soldiers were on. She plopped down onto a log, and tried to be as still as possible until the soldiers had ran past her. She let out a slow, long breath.

She looked down at herself, disgusted; and tried to comb her hair frivolously with her hands. Of course that didn't help much at all. She gave up with a small sigh in acceptance and laid down on the moist green forest floor pushing the log out of the way. She put her hands behind her head and gazed up at the endless blue sky. An unexpected sense of peace came upon her. She could hear the distant sounds of nature- the swooshing of the leaves, the buzzing of the insects… That's when she suddenly realized something was crawling under her. To her surprise, though, she didn't care, or maybe she was too tired to.

As the princess of an Aztec village, she was always properly dressed in perfectly clean attire and smelled fresh with the gentle scent of lavender that she loved so much. Her mother would always put sprigs of lavender in her chest of drawers. The villagers also believed that lavender would bring good luck. It was just another one of their many superstitions, but it meant a lot to the girl. She missed that smell; that feeling of cleanliness.

Her family had been living in the same village for centuries, and her ancestors ruled the land before the Americans took most of it away. Her ancestors managed to hang on to the small village where the girl lived with her family for as long as she could remember.

The girl was kind, caring and extremely polite, but you couldn't miss that defiant, rebellious spark in her eyes. As a relatively large scorpion made its way up her chest and towards her chin, she held her breath and tried to remain still. The scary bug had bright yellow eyes and a pitch black, six-inch long tail with a razor sharp stinger that could penetrate her skin in a split second. It would be a matter of minutes before her death after that. Still, she did not move or make a sound. The scorpion slowly crawled its way back from the girl's chest, down her arm to the forest floor, and slowly stumbled away. She let out a muddled sigh of relief.

Bees, flies, and the millions of different species of insects made increasingly loud and aggravating buzzing and hissing sounds as they flew around the girls head, but she was oddly at peace with it all. She knew that what she had done could possibly destroy their ancient civilization, and cause the dictator to wreak havoc on her village. Still, she knew it was the right thing to do given the circumstances. She felt it deep in her bones. After all, she had something that the dictator wanted. She chuckled, thinking to herself. He would love to get his hands on it. He'd probably do almost anything.

"WHERE IS THAT GIRL?!" The scream caused the ground to shake with its amazing power.

THE LOST JEWEL

"K-king Zala... We are still not sure of her whereabouts, s-sir."

"MOOP! YOU WORTHLESS PIECE OF TRASH! WHY HAVEN'T YOU FOUND HER?! ANSWERS! ANSWERS ARE WHAT I NEED!" The king's yelling caused a group of soldiers to come bursting into the throne room, mumbling words of care to the king in an attempt to calm him down. Moop, the king's assistant, shivered in fear.

"Sir, it's just... w-we need more time, y-your highness..." Moop whimpered.

"I WILL HAVE NONE OF THAT! GUARDS, BRING ME VAJRA LOKCIC! WE WILL FIND HIS DAUGHTER..." Zala screamed. The king took a deep breath, and broke out into a creepy smile.

"...At all costs."

"Yes, y-your highness." Moop replied indignantly. As he hurried away to do his job, the guards stopped him and Zala exclaimed,

"Moop, how many times do I have to tell you! You are not a soldier!"

"Oh, right. So sorry, sir, King Zala, sir." Moop whispered the apology, shaking. The king smiled at his fear. He loved it.

"I do have a job for you, though."

"Of course, your highness! Anything!"

THE LOST JEWEL

"Go wash the toilets. GUARDS!" The soldiers in the back stomped up, pushing Moop out of the way, who ran to begin his assignment.

"I have a strong feeling Vajra will know exactly where to find Alissa… If I'm right, we will have her in no time and our plan will be complete!"

"YESSIR!" The guards stomped out in a synchronized march. Once the last soldier left the room, King Zala sunk into his chair. He looked around at his throne room. The walls were painted a pristine white that seemed to glimmer in the sunlight coming in from the gigantic oval-shaped windows that resided on the two opposite walls. His red velvet throne was placed in the center of the adjacent wall with a long red velvet carpet leading all the way to the entrance of the room. A silver bejeweled crown was embedded on the top of the chair. King Zala couldn't help but grin at the thought of what he'd do to Vajra once his soldiers brought him to the castle.

"Where are you, Alissa?"

"Honey, where is she?"

"I don't know… I just don't know." Vajra tried to calm down his wife and wipe the tears from his younger daughter's eyes as he tended to the many burns that plagued her arms and legs. He wondered how he was going to fix all this himself. Since King Zala took over the town, the villagers considered Vajra a rebellion leader, and it was up to him to end the madness. The only thing stopping him from thinking straight was the fact that his own daughter had caused the destruction, and he didn't even know how it happened. The family sat in a small meadow a few hundred yards away from the village; to get away from the carnage of the forest surrounding it and the burned down houses. The three of them were sitting on a fallen tree trunk.

"Daddy?" The girl whimpered, tears falling from her dirty cheeks.

"Yes, Lela?"

"Are we going to be okay?"

"I hope so… I hope so."

Inside the metallic room of The Factory, the whole group looked discouraged. Gwen sat in the corner facing the wall, her hands covering her face. She had been like that for at least two hours, and nothing could make her move. Peter and Annie were sitting at the table, as were Trevor, Emily, and Dan. All of them had solemn and deeply hopeless looks on their faces.

"Dan…" Peter mumbled, his eyes cloudy with sadness.

"Yeah, what's up?"

"What are we going to do now?" Suddenly, Trevor jumped up from his seat.

"Okay, I know I'm not the best when it comes to high-pressure situations, but I think it would be best if Peter,

Dan, and I went to find him." Trevor said this with such clarity that everyone was taken aback.

"…Alright then. You guys should go find him. I'm… Not in the mood. It's a long story, okay?" Annie muttered, turning away from the group awkwardly.

"I want to help find Kr —I mean, him," Emily began to chime in before Gwen turned around viciously to face the group, stomped her feet and exclaimed,

"You can say his name! We all know you're talking about Kris!" With that, she pouted and went back to her corner, letting herself fall onto the cold, hard, metallic floor with a loud thud. Her head swiveled back around for a moment to make sure no one saw her fall.

Dan was watching in subtle amusement, but subconsciously he was deeply worried about his friend, Kris, like all the others. Throughout his adventures to find his parents, Dan knew he couldn't have accomplished anything without Kris' help. Just thinking about him made Dan want to punch something. After all, he blamed himself for letting those evil men get away with him. It was hard to comprehend the fact that in this very bizarre, metallic room where they had all been, not too long ago, training for a journey surrounding his own life, they were now brainstorming ways to save him from the clutches of evil.

THE LOST JEWEL

"We have to do something *now*, Dan. Don't you agree?" Emily asked, getting Dan's attention by poking him and gesturing to the girls in the room.

"I suppose. You guys don't have to do anything, though. None of you do. This… this is my fault. And I'm going to fix it, whether all of you come along with me or no one." The group nodded solemnly. A silence fell; not a single word was uttered for a solid minute when George came bursting through the door, startling everyone.

"So, I have some bad news. It's not about Kris. Well, I have some news about him too."

As the group waited anxiously, Gwen spoke up, running to the professor, "What do you know about Kris?" She yelled, tugging his lab-coat enthusiastically.

"Well, we may have a clue as to his whereabouts. Nothing is certain, though." This made Gwen's face light up immediately.

"Hey, what's the other news?" Dan pondered. Everyone swiveled their eyes back at the professor. His smiling face turned grim as he spoke.

"Well, I've had a talk with your parents, Dan, and due to the nature of their jobs, they have some connections, and…"

"Yeah, yeah, that's great, what is it?!" Annie snapped. Professor George hesitated before responding slowly.

"We have to save the world…"

THE LOST JEWEL

The forest seemed to get muggier and thicker as the night came upon Alissa, and she was fully aware of this as she trudged through wet shrubs and foliage. Using her pocket knife, she viciously hacked at the annoying leaves covering the path, wiping sweat from her brow. This was not the life made out for the young princess, and she knew that now more than ever before. She didn't stop slashing and moving until she felt it. At first it was just one drop, innocently placing itself atop her head.

"Rain."

Wasting no time, Alissa hurried to create a comfortable place to stay for the night under a gigantic tree that shielded her from the weather. The rain had begun to fall violently now, and she was relieved she found somewhere to take shelter, even if she was still technically out of the open. She tried to validate taking a break by reasoning that it had been getting dark and she would have stopped to sleep anyway.. She gathered some of the softer leaves she could find nearby and set this nature pillow next to the trees' trunk. Alissa laid her head down and started to doze off; her eyes fluttering with exhaustion. She had almost fallen asleep when she heard it - the loud, unmistakable crunch of feet walking over a dead branch. Alissa's eyes shot open and her body froze. At this time of night, who knows what was out there? She scanned her surroundings for a clue, but there was nothing but typical jungle plants. Not satisfied,

Alissa remained motionless for another minute. More crunching and shuffling noises came, until she saw them— two big yellow eyes glaring back at her in the middle of a bush. Her gasp wasn't audible, but her blood was racing so fast she could hear it. Adrenaline coursing through her veins, she didn't dare move. She thought to herself, so this is how it ends… A jaguar mauling in the middle of the night stranded in a jungle. Seems fitting. In the next moment, the mysterious creature's eyes were gone from sight. Alissa, still frozen, looked around slowly. No sign of the animal, or any more noises. Her muscles relaxed and she placed her head back on the pillow again, scratching at the top of her head as her hair had suddenly become itchy.

"Chii!'

"AAHHH!"

Alissa screamed in fear as she threw the animal resting on her head to the ground.

"A lemur?"

The creature lay on the jungle floor, whimpering with a sad look on its face. Alissa sat next to it, instantly feeling guilty for her violent actions. She petted its tiny head, softly at first. She realized the animal had no intention to hurt her. She picked the lemur up and set it in her lap, cuddling it. The lemur cooed in response.

"You're so cute… I think I'll name you Jo."

"Jo!"

"You catch on fast, little guy!" The lemur squeaked in delight, clapping its little paws. This made Alissa laugh, and then they both felt the fatigue of the day. Yawning, Alissa settled down into her makeshift bed and pulled Jo next to her.

"Good night, Jo."
"Jo!"

CHAPTER 2: Costly Fault

"Could you get the door, Lela?" The girl nodded, skipping through the small home. When she opened the door, she let out a sharp yelp of fear.

"Is this the home of Vajra?" Two soldiers stood at the entrance of the Lokcic family, their uniforms shining from the bright, overbearing sun.

THE LOST JEWEL

Lela didn't say a word before Vajra came to the door behind her.

"Yes, I'm here. I'm ready go, just give me a moment." Then the man, so tired from the past few days, kneeled down to get to Lela's height and looked into her worried green eyes. He put his hand on her cheek, speaking to her in a soothing tone.

"Lela, they need me to answer some questions about your sister. I'll be back before you know it, okay? Take care of mommy for me, sweetie."

"U-uh." Lela, still unable to talk coherently, nodded slowly, wiping a tear from her face and sniffling. The soldiers muttered among themselves awkwardly. Vajra stood, adjusting his clothing and giving his youngest daughter a weak smile.

"I'll be back as soon as I can." The door shut behind him as he left, leaving Lela with a sorrow that no stuffed animal in the world could fill.

Vajra stood in front of the headquarters. It was pitch black, smack in the middle of the village that his family called home. It had spikes jutting out the top and an image of a hawk was painted to the front of the building. It stuck out like a sore thumb from the rest of the architecture.

"In here," the soldiers said, pushing Vajra forward. They entered the building and the soldiers led Vajra to the main room, where king Zala was waiting.

THE LOST JEWEL

"You are to enter this room and answer King Zala's questions honestly. Resistance will be futile." A pause from the soldier.

"And deadly." Silence.

"You may enter."

Vajra, shaking from fear, swallowed harshly and opened the large door to reveal the long red carpet. Vajra had heard many tales of the people Zala had slain on this very red carpet.

"Ah, yes. Welcome, Vajra." The voice made him cringe. That same voice had rung through the village, explaining plans of death and destruction to the citizens.

"Welcome to hell."

"What do you want, Zala?" Vajra snapped, trying not to look the king in the eye.

"You shall refer to me as King Zala, village scum. Do not force me to order my soldiers to attack you." The dictator hissed. Vajra said nothing.

Compared to Vajra, the king looked like one of the richest men on the planet. He was suited with a shining white cape with a red fur outline. His suit was bright purple with red lines on the sleeves, and his black shoes matched the infinitely dark and dreary shade of the building itself. Vajra's rags that he had on and dark brown scruff on his face looked petty compared to the king's bold blonde curly locks.

"I have nothing to tell you, *King* Zala," Vajra told him, turning away angrily.

THE LOST JEWEL

"You lie!" The king exclaimed, slamming his fist into his chair. King Zala's face was bright red with anger.

"You're Alissa's father, you must know where she would have gone at a time like this! Tell us now, and we won't make your loved ones pay for your inability to comply." This made Vajra worried. Images of Lela's face flashed in his mind.

"King Zala, you don't understand, I have no idea why my daughter did this! Alissa is a nice girl! She never told me what she was plotting against you, all-powerful one!" Vajra got on his knees, bowing down to the dictator, who was now smirking.

"Very cute. Now you try to be a loyal villager, huh? That doesn't work anymore, Vajra!" King Zala's voice erupted. Vajra shivered on the floor, trying to remain clam.

"Powerful lord, if I knew anything of this evil plan to thwart you, I would let you know immediately. I know nothing. This is not a lie." Vajra pleaded, looking up at the king with scared eyes.

"Please… spare my family..." Although Zala knew Vajra was telling the truth, it was not enough.

"Moop!"

"Yes, my king!" On cue, the assistant came sprinting down the hall, two ferrets inside his left hand and a sandwich in the other. His pants were pulled down exposing his undergarments and he had a red substance on his face.

"Before I ask anything about your horrid appearance, escort Vajra here to the dungeon. We shall keep him captive until Alissa is found and it is secured."

"Yes sir!" Moop saluted the king, clumsily dropping his sandwich in the process. As he knelt to pick it up, the ferrets bit his hand, causing him to shriek and release them from his grasp. The two creatures ran rampant through the room, biting anything that moved and nibbling on furniture.

"MOOOOOOP!" The king's face was so similar to a tomato at this point one might mistake it for one.

"Sir, I-I'm terribly sorry!" Moop whimpered, running after the rascals.

"I want you…and those critters… Out of my sight. NOW."

"Of course, sir. Sorry, sir."

"Enough 'sir'! Just. Leave!" Without another word, Moop scurried out of the room, having captured the two ferrets. In a second, he came back, blushing, and grabbed Vajra's arm. Finally, the two made their way to the dungeon. King Zala sighed.

"With help like this, it'll be a miracle if we ever find this girl…"

"Sir? If I may?" A soldier cautiously stepped forward from his post.

"What is it, Henry"

"I'm John. That fellow over there is Henry." John pointed to a man in identical armor from across the room.

"Right. What is it, John?" King Zala corrected himself, shaking his head.

"Well... What is the importance of the girl? We know she set the village on fire, but... You planned to do that in the first place. Not exactly, but destruction of the area was certainly on your agenda, at some point. So... What is the real reason?" King Zala's expression changed. Suddenly, he didn't seem to be quite so angry. With a slight grin, the dictator responded.

"John, there are things behind the scenes that are more important than your entire life at stake here. I suggest you never step out of line by asking me such a preposterous question again if you value your job." That shut the soldier up. He returned to his post, and an eerie silence fell over the room.

Moop led Vajra down a narrow set of stairs covered in mold and dirt, away from the polished rooms of the rest of the building. The stairs seemed endless, and Moop felt the need to fill the silence.

"So, Vajra, do you really have no idea what Alissa has done?"

"I have no clue, and I also do not know why it is so important to you and your leader," Vajra replied angrily, trying to clear the steps as quickly as possible.

"Well, I'm not supposed to tell you..." Moop looked behind them to see if anyone was following, and as they reached the end of the stairs, he explained.

THE LOST JEWEL

"The real reason King Zala took over your silly village isn't to devastate your lifes. There is a hidden item that is priceless to any man in the entire world—a jewel that can only be found here; worth millions and millions of dollars, hidden away in this village.

"Zala planned to tear this village apart to have an easier time looking for it, but to his great surprise, the burning commenced the night before he planned to, and not by anyone under his rule. The culprit was your daughter, Alissa. King Zala and his supporters have agreed that this act must mean one thing."

"And what's that, Moop?" Vajra turned to him, his eyes tired with confusion and dread. Moop chuckled, as if it was too obvious, even for someone of his intellectual ability.

"Alissa has the jewel!"

A needle could be heard if it were dropped on the floor in the cold metal room. George's worried expression didn't ease anyone's nerves either.

"...You have seriously got to be kidding me," Trevor wasn't the only one in disbelief. Dan, speechless, turned away while running his fingers through his hair. Emily and Annie sighed, shaking their heads, while Gwen was unresponsive. Peter and Annie were the first to ask the question on everyone's minds, however.

"What are we going to have to do now?"

"Well, it's hard to explain." George was still standing, his lab coat reaching all the way to the floor as it was several sizes too big.

"We have all the time in the world. Sit down and tell us," Peter gestured for the professor to sit.

"See, that's ironic. Because we don't. Marv's waiting outside The Factory."

"What?!" Dan jumped at the sound of his beloved griffin's name.

"Yes! So I'll explain everything on the way there, we must get going now!" Professor turned and started to leave the room, when Gwen squeaked from her corner,

"Where are we even going?"

"South America, darling!" George winked at her, a trademark crooked smile on his face.

Alissa woke up alone. She vaguely remembered meeting a nice lemur the night before and sleeping with it in the rain. Shrugging, she decided it must've been a dream and got up to stretch her limbs.

"Chii-chii!" Alissa turned around, startled, to see her furry companion with a handful of brightly-colored fruits. Jo smiled up at her, and dropped two of the fruits near her foot. Picking them up curiously, Alissa held the food up to the light, exaggerating her inspection of them for Jo's amusement.

"Hmm... Are you trying to poison me, Jo? Will I be dead in five minutes?" Concerned, Jo violently shook his little head, muttering noises of dissent.

"Okay. I'll save these for later, but thank you." Alissa knelt down to Jo's level and patted the creature's head, causing him to coo happily. Before Alissa could get the chance to straighten herself again, Jo crawled up her arm and took a position on her shoulder.

"If that's what you want," Alissa laughed. Before leaving, she made sure she had all her belongings.

"Alright then, onward!" In a gesture mocking a drill sergeant, Jo pointed forward to the deeper end of the jungle. The duo trudged on, Alissa again using her pocketknife to make a path for her and her newfound companion. Jo tugged at her shirt and looked at her with a confused expression.

"Are you wondering where we're going, Jo?" The lemur nodded.

"Well... I don't have an answer." Alissa stopped. She was silent for a moment. Where *was* she going? Nowhere, she thought. Well, nowhere in particular. There wasn't an answer. The jungle seemed endless. Alissa started to say something, but then she realized something.

"Chi?" Jo tilted his head in a questioning matter, but Alissa had nothing to say. She was running away from the problem. She had left her family, her village, her life, in ruins, and for what? For a good cause, she told herself, to save the jewel, but where was she going to put it? She couldn't keep it forever and she certainly couldn't leave it anywhere in the jungle. This running away from the village was useless. All she was doing was making the problem worse. Going back now would be even worse than staying put. King Zala would get the jewel, and the villagers would have nowhere to live as she'd left the place in ruins. To make matters worse, with the jewel in the wrong hands, the possibilities were endless. She had to make a decision. She must continue on. She felt a pang of guilt as she saw, in her mind's eye, her beloved sister sprawled on the jungle floor, right outside her flaming home, her face coated with dirt and blood and her parents nowhere to be found. The look on Lela's face was like a stab to the heart, and Alissa couldn't help but cry, tears beginning to stream from her face. She shook her head violently, trying to get the vision out of her mind, out of her body, but the feeling that had struck her so deeply seemed to stick to her bones like glue. Jo, thoroughly worried for his new friend, poked her dirty cheek and cooed silently in a comforting tone. Alissa was grateful for her furry friend. Alissa gathered herself and wiped the tears from her cheeks. She had to keep moving.

"Come on, Jo," she muttered, her voice cracking. She still didn't know where she was going, but she knew she couldn't stop now.

Marv's gigantic red wings were always a sight to behold – they were long, majestic, and they gleamed in the sunlight. Dan walked over to his head, and patted his beak slowly.

"How've you been, old chap?" The bird chirped happily.

"I've been fine, Marvin. Thanks for asking," Dan responded, a grin appearing on his face for the first time in a while. The rest of the group said their hellos, and George gathered them all in front of Marv's right side.

"Okay, now I've been thinking, and I think it will be helpful to all of us if Peter and I stay at The Factory while the rest of you go." George waited for consent, but got the complete opposite.

"No way!" Emily yelled.

"Yeah, George, we stick together." Dan raised an eyebrow at Peter and Annie after saying that. Peter stepped in, looking straight at Dan with an emotionless face.

"You're right, Dan. But there's already a lot of us and you might need us back here to look up important information in the books. If you ever need us, you can call us and we'll come and help." He came over to Dan and put his hand on his shoulder.

"Yeah, we're always together—in our hearts," Annie added, smiling grimly at the group.

"I'm fine with that!" Gwen clapped her hands, motioning to Emily, Trevor, and Dan.

"Let's get a move on!"

"Are we all set?" Trevor asked George, who nodded.

"Your cell phones are in Marv's pouch, along with food, water, and other tools you may need on your journey." Trevor nodded, and let Emily go on first before hoisting Gwen onto the griffin's back. George pulled Dan aside before he could mount Marv. He looked him straight in the eyes, and waited a moment before he spoke.

"Dan, times have been tough, I know. But we've gotten through so much. We've stopped this evil organization once. We can do it again. Now go be a hero!"

"I will, George Juniper," Dan answered, smiling. George flashed his signature smile and backed up, allowing Marv to spread out his illustrious wings.

"Hey George, where in South America are we going?" Emily yelled as the flaps of Marv's wings muted the rest of the world out. Although the professor could not be heard, Marv responded.

"We're going to the wonderful country of Brazil, my friends. Hang on tight!"

"Always do!" Dan yelled back, winking at Gwen, who giggled in response. The little girl gasped when she felt the sensation of Marv's talons releasing from the earth below them. Dan wrapped his arms around her and said,

"Don't worry, I got you." Gwen smiled back at him and at that point, they were the most happy they've been in a long time.

THE LOST JEWEL

Moop was hungry. As he walked back up the narrow stairs to the main rooms of the building, he groaned as his stomach rumbled longingly. His eyes darted to the door of the kitchen, and he made his way over. He was about to open the door when he heard voices. Moop froze.

"King Zala, what is worrying you so? The girl will eventually figure out there's nothing she can do and come back to us. Even if she doesn't, the jungle doesn't reach all over the world. At some point she'll be in a place where we can capture her," one of King Zala's henchmen was talking.

"Bailey, you don't understand. Once we capture the girl and the jewel, we'll have bigger fish to fry." This confused Bailey, as Moop could tell by the pause in his voice.

"But, sir, I thought you were forming a dictatorship over the village, and then the rest of South Ame-"

"Bailey! Why can't you comprehend this?!" King Zala interrupted, slamming his fist on the table.

"This mission is just a stepping stone. Once we have the jewel we won't be staying in this junkyard for any longer. We'll be going to larger, more important cities, where we can use it to take over stronger communities until we've taken hold of the world!" King Zala chuckled, his evil smirk making Bailey uncomfortable.

"Yes, my lord, that sounds like a wonderful plan. But, what of…"

"The Factory workers? You know the plan, of course, Bailey."

"Umm…" The assistant looked down, his face a bright red shade that emanated embarrassment

"Of course not. Heaven forbid the people here don't know what's going on…" King Zala muttered under his breath angrily, shaking his head. With a cynical tone, the dictator explained.

"To stop them from annoying us andruining our plans, we're going to sell it like our home base is here, and once we lure them in with Kris, we'll board the ships and escape to Europe. It's perfect!" King Zala clapped his hands excitedly.

"There's one problem, my king," Bailey mumbled, his eyes avoiding King Zala's.

"And what would that be?" King Zala's snarky voice seemed to mock Bailey; to coax out a cry of fear and make him run out of the room.

"Well… do you know how to navigate a ship, sir?"

"Very good, Bailey." King Zala walked over to the ingredient cabinet. Bailey, relieved that he hadn't gotten his head sliced off, sighed loudly and rested his side against the counter. King Zala picked up a bright red tomato, feeling its delicate skin and testing out its ripeness. His magnification with the fruit caused Bailey to prompt him.

"King Zala?"

THE LOST JEWEL

"Don't worry your worthless head about that, Bailey. We've got it under control." With that, King Zala took a knife and threw it across the room so suddenly that Bailey dropped to the floor, whimpering. The knife lodged itself into a cabinet on the opposite side of the room with a loud clang, and with a demonic laugh, King Zala left the room. Moop stood, star-struck, outside the kitchen, looking at the dictator with huge eyes.

"Moop, stop looking at me like that. Your ugly face is ruining my day."

"Of course, my lord," Moop answered, scampering into the kitchen. With King Zala out of sight, he ran over to Bailey and put his arm around him.

"Are you okay?" Moop asked, but he wasn't genuinely worried and as soon as he saw the knife stuck in the cabinet he became engulfed in it.

"Wow, did The King throw this? That's so cool!" Moop tried to pull the knife out of the cabinet, but to no avail. Bailey slowly stood up, shaking his head. He looked into Moop's eyes. They were so filled with wonder and excitement that there was no room for pain, and Bailey was jealous of that.

"I'm fine, Moop. Thanks for asking." The assistant left the kitchen without another word.

"More food for me!" Moop announced gleefully, skipping into the pantry to collect more food.

THE LOST JEWEL

The scenery was truly beautiful. Sure, there were pesky bugs that bit every inch of skin on your body and the vines that covered the floor of the jungle gripped and tugged at your ankles and opened wounds that you wouldn't notice until three hours later, but once you get past all that and the overwhelming heat, it really was gorgeous. The leaves and foliage created layers of greenery on top of each other in a succession that looked like a canvas splattered with different shades of green, while colorful splashes of fruits and berries covered the plants. The gigantic trees looming overheard shielding you from the deadly sun, and the trunks that seemed to be stronger than anything else in the jungle. There were so many spots that couldn't be seen, that could hold dangerous animals or plants, but Alissa still loved being in the jungle. There was a certain thrill to having to savor your life every second, and she felt it when she was in there. Jo was wrapped around her neck, munching on an extremely juicy yellow berry. Alissa laughed as Jo's bites caused droplets of berry juice to stick to her face. If this was how she was going to have to spend the next few weeks, she wouldn't mind that much at all. In the village, all she did was work and work. Not a moment to play, only gather provisions, build new houses, help out a sick child from another family. Never a moment to herself. Now she had all the time in the world, and she certainly relished it. She didn't mind the lemur's company either. He helped to pick out the fruits that weren't poisonous. Alissa began to talk to Jo as they walked, getting into the rhythm of her plant-hacking.

"So Jo, where do you come from?

"Chiiii!" Jo gave Alissa a roll of his big yellow eyes, indicating how stupid the question was. Alissa laughed and changed her question.

"Right. Uh, do you have any family in the jungle?" Jo smiled and nodded.

"Chi-chi-chi!"

"Three family members?" Jo nodded.

"How many children?" Alissa asked, and Jo held up both paws.

"So, two?" Jo nodded again, smiling. Suddenly, the lemur crawled on Alissa's back and purred slowly, as if he were depressed. Alissa frowned.

"What's wrong, Jo?" Alissa gently picked Jo up off of her back and held her up in front of her face. The lemur's eyes looked so much more serious than they had a minute ago that Alissa was taken aback. Then, she put it together.

"You miss your family, huh?" Jo nodded solemnly, cuddling his tail in his hands. Alissa felt a pang of guilt for taking the animal, but Jo would just leave if he didn't want to be in Alissa's company, and although she wanted to help him, Alissa had no way of knowing where Jo's family could possibly be. The jungle was far too vast to search for them, and as much as it hurt Alissa, there was nothing she could do.

"I'm sorry, buddy. It may not be much, but you've got me," Alissa soothed him, patting his head. The lemur smiled, and nodded. Crawling back up onto her shoulder, Alissa continued on. She was glad that she could help Jo feel better, but still could not escape the feeling that she was doing something wrong by taking him along with her. Jo poked at her cheek annoyingly, darting his eyes back and forth. An eyebrow raised, Alissa asked, "What's wrong this time, Jo?" As she said it, her heart stopped.

In the corner of her eye, she could just make out the snout of a pitch black creature looking back at them. Its vicious eyes glared from afar, piercing Alissa's soul with its intensity. Alissa didn't dare move, and Jo followed suit, not adjusting even a finger. The creature slowly, almost sluggishly, made its way around a bush and seemed to be completely covered by a tree trunk. In an instant, the animal darted from the tree to a cluster of vines reaching to a branch of another tree. Its majestic body was in Alissa's full sight now, and she was frozen by its deadly beauty. It had a sleek mane that glistened in the sunlight as it moved, and its claws gleamed. It could attack at any moment. The staring match went on for what felt like hours; no one moved. The panther bared its sharp teeth at Alissa, who gulped. Jo made the slightest movement and whispered into Alissa's ear.

"Chi?"

"It'll be okay… Just don't move." Alissa made sure to keep her voice as low as possible, and at the same time calm Jo down. Their lives were at stake. At first glance the animal seemed extremely vicious, but after a few minutes of complete silence and no movement, the creature seemed less and less dangerous. Alissa whispered to Jo,

"Maybe it isn't as bad as we thought-" at that moment, the jaguar knelt down in the position to pounce. The two seconds it took Alissa to comprehend this, and run at the speed of light into the jungle, was all it took for the jaguar to barely miss Jo's face as they whizzed past. Heart pounding as loud as an orchestra, Alissa looked left and right, seeking a place to hide in desperation. She couldn't outrun the jaguar for another two minutes, and in four minutes she would be dead. Her brain went into overtime, going over the different options in her head. That didn't take long because there weren't many; keep running and eventually die or find somewhere to hide in the next thirty seconds. Finally, she stopped running as she saw an odd formation near a bush to the left of her. She placed her foot on the odd area to figure out it was a camouflaged incline. Without hesitation she quietly slid down and scrambled to get behind the bush before the jaguar reached the clearing. Within seconds, the beast appeared, sniffing violently. Alissa held her breath and began to pray frantically, holding Jo tightly to her chest. The lemur knew not to make a noise either, but his eyes spoke a thousand words; the worry in them only deepening Alissa's fear. The pair watched intensely as the jaguar slowly made its way around the clearing. It took small, calculated steps. Alissa realized the creature was making its way in their direction. Sweating profusely, Alissa managed to not scream, trying to calm herself down. The jaguar stopped abruptly, right in front of the bush.

Please, please God, please let me live, please… Alissa trembled wildly. Her heart was about to explode.

After the longest minute in Alissa's life, the jaguar leaped away, and in a few seconds the beast was gone, leaving Alissa and Jo alone. Both of them let out huge sighs of relief, smiling. They were still alive. The tension lifted from Alissa's shoulders and she got up and stepped forward, only to yell in shock when she suddenly began to roll downward, accelerating as she crashed into branches and other foliage. Jo, startled, ran after her as she fell down the hill. With a loud crunch, she finally stopped moving in a pile of drying leaves. She rolled over, groaning in pain, when her foot hit something cold and hard. Confused, she pulled back quickly. She motioned Jo to come closer and began moving leaves out of the way to reveal a rusty metal door, and on the front a label read:

"DO NOT OPEN – KING ZALA PROPERTY"

CHAPTER 3: Behind The Scenes

Once Alissa pulled the door open with the help of Jo, she heaved it to one side and climbed the ladder down the ensuing corridor. Jo followed suit, and once they reached the bottom he resumed his position on Alissa's shoulder. The air had a rotting smell to it and the greenish walls seemed to be sagging somewhat. The room was small and looked as if no one had been inside for years. Putting her hand over her nose to block out the disgusting stench, Alissa walked to a door that was in the corner. She tried to open it, but the door was locked. Stumped, she stepped back. What was this place? She couldn't think of any ideas. She tried to remember anything her father might've told her about a place like this. Maybe provisions? Jo lightly poked her in the shoulder, and directed Alissa's attention to a ring of keys on a knob near the entrance.

"Thanks, Jo!" The lemur giggled. Alissa went to get the key, and unlocked the metal door. Inside was an even longer corridor with narrow walls that Alissa and Jo could barely fit between. Turning to one side, they inched their way through until they came to another door, and began to open it when they heard a noise. Alissa quickly pushed the door open and Jo followed behind her. After closing it behind them, she waited for another sound. Footsteps were coming in the direction of the room they were in.

"So what do you think the king's gonna do with him?"

"I know as much as you know, bro."

"I thought you went to college?"

The two guards finally left the corridor, and Alissa and Jo got out of the room just as the guards turned the corner. Sighing, Alissa and Jo continued down the narrow corridor, more cautiously this time. They came across a gate with a number code, but the guards had left it open. Knowing that meant they'd be back soon, Alissa grabbed Jo and held him in her arms while she ran inside. Laying in a rusty jail cell before her was a small boy, about six years of age, with messy black hair and raggedy clothes. His body was grimy and he looked weak; he was sprawled out on the ground and groaning softly. Scars covered his arms and legs and his eyes were red and puffy. The boy looked up at Alissa and Jo slowly, obviously trying not to move too much of his body. Before Alissa could say anything, the boy spoke.

"Did you see a gun when you came in?"

Taken aback, Alissa replied,

"Why would you need a gun?" Rolling his eyes as if it was obvious, the boy responded.

"It's not that type of gun. A weapon that resembles a gun."

"…I don't know. I can go back and look."

"It should be in the room nearby," the boy mumbled, rolling over on the floor. Alissa began to head back to the room when she heard footsteps again. Jo whimpered, and Alissa quickly began to try and hide. There was no place to do that, though—the jail cell was the only thing in the room and nothing was hidden inside there.

"Hey, over here," the boy motioned for the duo to come in his direction.

"My name's Kris, by the way," he said as he fished something shiny out of his pocket and handed it to Alissa.

"This is an invention from The Factory, click the button on top and you'll be safe," Kris explained as the steps came closer and closer. Alissa nodded. A few seconds before the guards came into the room, Alissa pressed the button and closed her eyes. Nothing had changed. She was still in the room with Jo and could see the guards entering the room. However, after a couple of moments, Alissa realized something. They couldn't see her. The circular shiny object had made them invisible so that the guards had no idea of their presence.

"How you doin', Factory scum?" The guards chuckled, using a stick to poke at Kris' motionless body. He grumbled back,

"Great. You should let me go."

"Ha, nice try kid. We're not letting you out until the boss says so," one of the guards smirked, wagging his fingers in a mocking manner. Kris grunted, trying to get up. It was no use. All he could do was lay down and whimper in pain.

"We'll bring you food in an hour. Don't die while we're gone," the guard remarked, and the two burst out laughing as if it was the funniest thing ever said. They made their way down the corridor, their obnoxious laughing ringing through the building. The door shut, and Kris spoke immediately.

"Now press the button again." Alissa did so, and suddenly she could see her arms and legs again. She looked at Kris, who had a faint smile on his face.

THE LOST JEWEL

"Amazing, isn't it? The professor has some of the most innovative inventions in the world," his voice cracked, a tear falling from his eye.

"Hey, what's wrong?" Alissa asked. She kneeled down and put her arm around Kris. His eyes were full of pain; it made him seem much older than he was.

"I just… miss my family, that's all," he sniffed, trying to maintain his composure. In his maturity with handling the situation before, Alissa had forgotten how young he probably was.

"Aw, it's going to be okay," she tried to comfort him. She had no idea who the professor was, or The Factory, but she did know that this boy saved her, and the least she could do was soothe him.

"Chi Chi!" Jo exclaimed, and before Alissa could stop him, he lay on Kris' head and hugged him. Kris laughed, sitting up and petting Jo's back. He reached into his pocket and took out a tiny piece of bread. He ripped a bit off and gave it to Jo, who accepted it gleefully. After a minute of silence, Kris looked up at Alissa.

"Do you think you could help me get out of here?" Kris asked hopefully.

"I would love to help you, but uh…" Alissa stammered, "I don't know what to do."

"I'll walk you through it, don't worry. Will you help?" Kris asked again. His confidence convinced Alissa in a heartbeat,

"Gladly. What first?" Alissa asked. The room remained empty. Kris' eyes were constantly scanning behind them, making sure no guards were about to enter.

"First, you need to get my bag. I think they put it in that cabinet over there." Kris pointed to a metal cabinet on the wall on the other side of the room.

"And there's probably a key to that then?" Alissa asked, examining the cabinet.

"Right. That's the hard part. You're going to have to take a key from one of the guards," Kris explained, watching Alissa and Jo carefully. Without a word, Alissa nodded.

"Good. They all go to a lounge around this time. When you first entered this secret area, did you see a door right around the corner from the ladder?"

"I didn't look there, but I can go back and check."

"Okay, once you find that door, you're going to have to use the contraption I gave you again. Press the button, and then open the door. If you can, make some obnoxious noises to draw the guards out. Hopefully one of them will leave their keys inside. Go in and grab them, and come back here. Simple and easy," Kris chuckled.

"Gotcha! Be back soon!" Alissa exclaimed, walking out of the room. Jo turned and gave Kris a wink before they left. Alissa walked down the corridor quickly with Jo firmly attached to her shoulder, and stopped at the entrance. She found the ladder again and walked around the corner to the left. She spotted the room Kris had described and peeked inside the window. There were four guards talking around a roundtable, laughing and drinking. Alissa looked at Jo, who pressed the button on the contraption to make them invisible. Alissa creaked the door open and Jo let out an ear piercing screech.

"CHI CHI CHI CHI!" Startled, the guards jumped out of their seats and ran to the door. They hurried down a corridor to the far left, not in Kris' direction, and once they were out of sight, Alissa went into the lounge. She looked around frantically for a set of keys, but there were none. She could already hear the guards coming back, empty-handed and angry. Without much time to think of a better option, Alissa crawled under the round table and held Jo tight to her chest. For the second time today, the two held their breaths for their lives, hoping the guards wouldn't notice them. As the four sat back down again, Alissa noticed that the keys were linked to their belts, and all four of them had an identical set. Alissa got Jo's attention, and pointed to the keys. Jo nodded, and slowly made his way to one of the guards sides.

"Wonder what that was, huh?" One guard remarked, putting his legs up on the table.

"Probably one of the animals up there becoming lunch," another joked, and the group laughed.

"I can almost smell one in here now!" A third said, and Alissa and Jo both froze. The man that said that was the same one that Jo was right next to. The guard's facial expression changed, and he looked down straight at Jo. His eyebrow raised, he lowered his head until his eyes were inches away from Jo's. Alissa was surprised they had not heard her heart yet as it was pounding louder than ever. She gulped as another guard spoke.

"Everything okay?" After another minute, the guard sat back up and responded.

"Yeah, I thought I felt something around my leg. Guess it was just my imagination." Both Alissa and Jo sighed, relieved that they hadn't been found out. Now it was the matter of retrieving a set of keys. Alissa motioned for Jo to continue on, and the lemur nodded back at her. He began to make his way of the chair, careful not to come in contact with the guard, until he was right next to the keys. Suddenly, the door slammed opened, and a man walked in.

"Bailey! What are you doing here?" One of the guards asked the man. Unknown to Alissa, the man had a slight beard and dirty blonde hair. He seemed to be in his late twenties, and sported a royal robe that was caked in mud and dirt. He sighed, his eyebrows furrowed.

"Do you have… any idea… how long it took me… to find this place…?" Bailey heaved, and one of the guards hurried over to fetch him a glass of water and a chair. The man dropped into the chair with a thud, downing the glass in just a matter of seconds. He looked around at the guards, who hadn't spoken a word.

THE LOST JEWEL

"…Sir, what brings you here?" One of the guards questioned.

"I've been sent to see how things are doing. Just a routine check-up is all," Bailey responded, swishing his hair back.

"Sir, your suit is a little…"

"Covered in grime? Yes, I noticed. Thanks to this place being so hidden I had to take a ride down that nasty hill." Bailey shuddered, attempting to dust off one of his sleeves. Both Alissa and Jo hadn't moved since Bailey arrived.

"How's the Alissa hunt?" One of the guards asked, and the rest of them laughed. Alissa couldn't help it; the gasp came out before she could think to hold it in.

"What was that?" Bailey asked.

"I… don't know." One of the guards responded. Alissa was sure she was going to faint. The 'Alissa Hunt' could be over before they knew it, thanks to her stupidity.

"…Hmm…" Bailey mumbled, pacing slowly around the room. Alissa tried to tell Jo not to move without speaking, and he got the message. If anything happened to ruin their cover, Alissa would be brought back in and she couldn't bear to think about the things King Zala would do to her when she got there. Suddenly, Bailey kneeled down and looked under the table. Alissa's heart, for the second time, stopped inside of her as his eyes looked through her invisible body. After a minute, Bailey stood back up, dusted his shirt off, and nodded at the guards.

"Alright. Looks like everything is good here. I'll be off." With that, he turned to leave the room.

"Hey, tell King Zala we need a raise!" One of the guards chirped jokingly.

"I'll add it into my report," Bailey winked before leaving. Alissa signaled for Jo to take the keys at that moment, and as Bailey began to leave the room, Alissa and Jo made a dash for the door, squeezing behind him. Once Bailey had gone back up the ladder and the guards resumed their conversation, Alissa sighed with relief. Jo seemed to be just as emotionally drained.

"It's been a long day for us, huh buddy?" She laughed. The two began their walk back to Kris' jail cell.

"So I guess the king has warranted a search for me," Alissa said. Jo nodded, and turned his head questioningly.

"Chi?"

"I don't know… Let's just be grateful they didn't catch me this time," Alissa responded. She tried not to think about it, but her mind couldn't help but wander to her family. If this was how intensely Zala was searching for her, her family must be in serious danger. She clutched her most coveted possession in her shorts pocket. The one thing that the king wanted so desperately was in her hands, and she was determined to keep it out of his dirty, thieving ones. If it was the last thing she did, it would be to never let the king lay eyes on the gem.

But, Lela... Vajra... Alissa thought, mouth wavering. Jo crawled down Alissa's shoulder to where the gem was in her pocket, and pulled it out before Alissa could stop him. It was a regularly sized jewel, about the size of Jo's fist, and glowed a bright purple.

"Keep that in my pocket, Jo. If anyone sees it, the only thing it will bring is more trouble for us." The lemur grumbled at the thought of any more trouble after all they had been through and returned the gem to its original spot. Jo handed the key ring to Alissa once they reached the entrance to the cell room. Once inside, Alissa and Jo found Kris sleeping in the middle of the cell floor. The duo headed over to the cabinet and unlocked it, revealing a pitch black bag with two handles on either side. Alissa grabbed it and brought it over to the jail cell.

"Chi!" Jo squeaked, and pointed to the zipper of the bag furiously. With an eyebrow raised, Alissa opened the bag. Jo scampered in and pulled out a small metal hand-gun with a red tip. He pointed to the bars of the cell with both fingers and used them to create finger guns. Alissa giggled and nodded, and aimed the gun to the bar. The shot had no effect on Alissa, but the substance that came out of the gun caused the bar to instantly melt until it was a puddle of metal slush on the floor. Alissa gasped in awe.

"Who is this child?" she wondered aloud, turning the gun over in her hand. Alissa proceeded to take out four more bars until there was a wide enough gap for her to get through. Without hesitation, she entered the jail cell and hurried inside to wake Kris. His eyes fluttered open and he mumbled.

"Are we leaving, then?" He got up and dusted his clothes off. A cobweb awkwardly hung in his hair and he swatted it away. He glanced down at the puddle of metal at his feet and noticed his bag on the floor next to Alissa.

"Liking my gun?" He asked as Alissa blushed, handing him the weapon. The three of them hopped over the melted metal and Kris entered the code one last time to exit the room. As they made their way out, Kris remarked,

"You know, this place would have been nice if it didn't smell so bad." The three of them laughed, Jo happily perched on Alissa's shoulder. They reached the ladder, and heard the guards from the room around the corner.

"Alright, we gotta feed the kid, it's lunch time."

"Do we really have to?" One of the guards groaned sarcastically.

"King Zala wants him alive. In fact, he said it was extremely important that he was alive," Another answered, and the other guards mumbled agreement.

"Let's get out of here. Once they figure out I've escaped, word will get out and they'll send back up to lock down the area. We need to distance ourselves from this section of the jungle," Kris explained, and the group spent no time making their way up the rusty ladder. Once they reached the top, Jo jumped off of Alissa's shoulder and galloped in one direction.

"We should follow him, he knows this place better than the both of us," Alissa exclaimed, running after the lemur. Kris followed suit, and they disappeared into the greenery.

Back down in the hideout, the guards walked down the corridor of the cell room, making conversation and laughing. The guard in front entered the code and they went inside, only to find an empty jail cell. The cabinet was hanging open as well, with a key ring dangling in the handle. Speechless, the guards searched their belts for a key.

"Well, who doesn't have it?!" One guard yelled. They looked around.

"Hey, where's…" They realized the fourth guard was trying to sneak out of the room. He stammered,

"Guys, I don't know how this happened… Someone must have pick-pocketed me or something, but it wasn't me! You have to understand!"

"There's only one problem about that…" One of the guards grumbled angrily. "There's no one else in this area! Who else would've done it?!" This shut the fourth guard up. The remaining two guards took both of his hands and cuffed them.

"You gotta believe me!' The guilty guard looked at the first one with pleading eyes.

"I don't believe traitors. Boys, have him sent to King Zala... God knows what he'll do to you."

Moop was a jolly man. He barely spent five minutes a day in a worrisome state. When he was worrying, it was usually about whether or not King Zala would kill him in a fit of rage. Other than that, the man lived a very care-free life. He was fed well in the palace and had a nice room to himself next to the dictator. He was catered to his every need and his job was usually to shut up before King Zala shot his face into bits. Moop skipped down the stairs to check on Vajra, whistling a mellow tune.

"That's very annoying, you know," Vajra called from his jail cell. Moop stopped his whistling and came over to the prisoner.

"Sorry, sir! How's life in the dungeon?" He chuckled, going over the key ring.

"What are you doing in here?" Vajra questioned.

"Making you lunch!" Moop replied, walking into the kitchen on the other side of the room. Chopping could be heard all the way in the cell. Vajra shuddered at the thought of eating something that man had cooked, but was relieved when the king's assistant brought out a simple cheese sandwich and water. Vajra took it and chewed his first bite slowly, staring straight into Moop's eyes. At that moment, a thought came across Vajra's mind. He put his sandwich down on his bed rest, and laid on his bed, kicking his legs up and throwing his hands behind his head.

"So, Moop—how's life going for you?" Vajra asked.

"I'm doing great, thanks for asking!" Moop responded happily, plopping down in a wooden chair near the kitchen.

"That's good... How are things with King Zala?" Vajra tried to seem nonchalant, but his curiosity was getting the best of him. It was all he could stand not to outright ask him the questions he had to know the answer to.

"Well you know King Zala, he can be a pain but he's a delight to be around!" Moop chirped, fiddling with his hair.

"Made any progress in catching my daughter?" Vajra asked casually, picking at food in between his teeth.

"No, but we definitely will!" Moop clapped his hands, as if the thought excited him.

"I mean, what's it all for, anyway?" Vajra asked, trying to make it sound as casual and normal as possible. Moop responded, absorbed in trying to pick something out of his fingernails.

"Well she has the jewel! We've already searched every square inch of this village, and there's nothing here! She must have it, and once we have it, the King will be all set."

"Set for what?" Vajra asked.

"Well, the trip to Europe of course! Once we get the jewel, the king will send people to take the jewel!" Moop answered, smiling every time he got something out of his nails. Vajra couldn't contain his excitement at this important news.

"What's in Europe?"

"I have no idea, but the king must have a good reason! I mean, he does want to take over the world! Haha!" Moop chuckled, now busy getting bugs out of his shoe.

"Right," Vajra laughed nervously, trying to keep his cool. Now it seemed so obvious to him. Why else would the king want the jewel? It seemed he had solved the puzzle quicker than Moop himself.

"Thanks, Moop." He smiled at the king's assistant, who was so oblivious to what was going on that he had no idea he had been tricked into giving away valuable information.

"No problem, buddy! I'll see you later!" Moop skipped up the stairs, and Vajra waved goodbye. Moop made his way to the king's main room and decided to surprise the dictator with a tray of snacks. He turned to the kitchen and grabbed the nearest plate of food he could find, and returned to the king's room.

"My lord, some delicacies from the kitchen!" Moop bowed, placing the plate in front of the king.

THE LOST JEWEL

"Moop, where have you been? The king questioned, taking a cautious bite from the exotic looking cheese in front of him.

"Oh, just checking on the prisoner like you asked, sir!" Moop responded, grabbing a piece as well.

"And all you did was feed him, correct?" King Zala ventured, watching Moop closely. The assistant didn't notice the kings intensity and remained just as cheerful as before.

"Yes, and we talked about the plan as well! It was very nice, sir," Moop explained cheerfully, munching loudly on the food meant for the king.

"The plan?" King Zala prompted him, anger rising.

"Oh, yes! I told him about our plan to take the jewel to Europe!" Moop answered, licking his lips. His eyes suddenly shot open when he realized King Zala's anger.

"...My lord?"

"Why would you tell him? WHY?!" King Zala yelled, slamming his fist on the arm rest of his chair. He got up from his throne and walked over to a side of the room, shaking his head in disbelief. Moop was frozen next to the plate of food.

"He's locked up anyway, my lord, there's nothing he could do with the information-" Moop tried to save himself, but King Zala wasn't listening.

"Moop... If you screw up my plans any more, you won't be alive to see that jewel make it to Europe." The tension in the room could be cut with a knife.

"Yes, sir. It won't happen again, sir." Moop bowed multiple times, while trying to inch his way out of the room. King Zala straightened his jacket and fixed the creases, looking down at Moop with shame.

"King Zala!" A voice cried from outside the room. One of the guards opened the door and in came Bailey running frantically, huffing and puffing. Sweat was dripping from his brow as he spoke.

"You… have… no idea… how much I've… ran today…"

"What is it, Bailey?" King Zala snapped, and Moop stood up, trying to look as professional as the other guards.

"Kris has escaped, and I think I know who helped him…" Bailey gulped. A moment of silence.

"Alissa Lokcic." The tone that came out of the dictator's mouth sounded inhumane.

"ARRRRRGH! SEND ALL GUARDS! HUNT THEM DOWN AT ALL COSTS!" King Zala roared in a blood-curdling scream. With many nods and bows, the guards and Bailey hurried out of the room, leaving Moop and King Zala.

"My lord, I am so deeply sorry, if those fools hadn't—" Moop began, but King Zala held up a hand.

"I am about four seconds away from ripping your skull out of its socket. Moop, I suggest you clear out. Now." Without another word, the assistant scurried away. King Zala, now completely alone in his throne room, kneeled on the floor, looking up at the sky in a mixture of sorrow, confusion, and pure rage.

    The breeze felt great on Dan's face. He took it all in. Out in the open again, on another journey with his best friends. He looked over at Trevor and Emily, chattering on the other side of Marv's torso. Gwen was asleep right next to Dan, her breathing slow and small compared to the powerful gusts in the sky around them. Dan scooted as close to the edge of Marv as possible and looked down. The world below him was a completely different one than up in the sky; the miniscule buildings and civilizations so unimportant in the new environment.

    "It's quite magnificent, eh old chap?" The griffin said. Dan nodded, amazed by it all.

    "Marv, do you ever get tired of flying? It seems so… wonderful," Dan asked.

    "Of course not, my friend. It's a marvelous thing any day of the week," Marv responded in his regular know-it-all tone, and Dan chuckled mildly. He wasn't really listening anymore. The feeling of the crisp winds flowing through his fingers absorbed him and he became enchanted in the forest of clouds surrounding him. Puffy and gigantic, the harmless giants exploded on impact as Marv flew through them, and Dan laughed as felt the light splashes of precipitation. In that moment, it seemed as if there were no worries in the world. All Dan could feel was the amazing sensation of flight.

"There's a rather large bout of clouds up ahead. I could make a detour and swoop through them, for the fun of it?" Marv asked.

"Sounds amazing!" Dan answered, and hurried to wake Gwen up. He motioned for Trevor and Emily to pay attention.

"Guys, watch this!" Dan stood up on Marv's back, and gave a thumbs up to the griffin, and he flew straight towards the cloud. Dan held both his hands out, and closed his eyes. The instant that the clouds encased the griffin, Dan grabbed at the fluffy parts and painted them across his face.

"You look like Santa Claus!" Gwen giggled, and Dan nodded, mocking the Christmas icon.

"Ho ho ho!" He jeered, holding his imaginary belt and rubbing his imaginary belly.

"That's weak, Dan!" Trevor scoffed. Emily pushed him jokingly, and Trevor pretended to lose his balance and slip down Marv's torso.

"Trevor!" Emily yelped, but Trevor regained his spot and laughed, pushing Emily back.

"I was just kidding," Trevor explained, noticing that Emily hadn't seen the humor in it and looked concerned.

"Hey, Trevor." Dan called. "That was weak!"

"You asked for it, Dan!" He jumped at his friend, and the two of them rolled around on Marv's back, tussling and laughing. Gwen and Emily shook their heads.

"Boys," they exclaimed solemnly.

THE LOST JEWEL

"You two be good back there!" Marv called as they flew farther and farther up and away from the ground.

"Yeah, we know!" Trevor called back as they continued to brawl. Gwen turned to Emily with big eyes.

"Do you think we'll find Kris, Emily?"

"I think anything's possible, sweetheart!" Emily answered wholeheartedly. Gwen smiled and Emily returned the favor.

"How long will it take for us to get to Brazil?" Emily asked Marv.

"It'll be a while, so I suggest you kids find something to do," Marv responded, gliding into a clearing after the forest of clouds. Emily looked out into the sky, and Gwen poked her.

"Is something wrong?"

"Oh, no, I'm just… thinking," Emily mumbled, but Gwen knew that was a lie and pried further.

"What's up, Em?" Gwen asked, not budging. Emily sighed and responded.

"It's nothing, really. I just wonder what's going to happen after this journey's over."

"Well we go back home!" Gwen replied, grinning at the thought of it.

"I know, but… my home isn't yours." Emily shrugged, as if it didn't mean much, but it meant the world. Gwen knew what she was talking about, even at the tender age of six, and put her arms around Emily.

"Well you're my sister now, so you can't go!" Emily chuckled at this, grateful for Gwen's company.

"Thanks, Gwen. I would never," she exclaimed, and the two of them giggled, and transitioned to talk about happier things. Suddenly, a device on Dan's person vibrated loudly. Dan, startled, began searching his pockets for the source.

"George slipped that on you before you left. Had you been paying attention, you would have noticed," Marv explained. "It's a communicating device," the griffin continued. "Set the knob forward and a holographic image of the caller will appear." Dan did as he was told and out popped a static-infested bright blue holographic image of Professor George.

"Hello, Dan! How are things?" The professor seemed to be holding back a worried voice, and Dan was curious to know what was up, but played along with the scenario as it was.

"Everything's just great over here," He responded. "What about over there?" The professor laughed a nervous laugh, scratching his head and fidgeting constantly.

"Well, we've got some transmissions coming in from helpers in South America," The professor began to explain, but then his focus was deterred when Peter and Annie came over, waving but looking just as worried.

"What kind of transmissions?" Trevor asked, slowly placing his hand on his belt. The four of them all felt as if they were about to receive some news they won't be happy about, and the professor's nonsense was only acting as evidence for their concerns.

"Dan, our sources tell us that the people that have Kris are the bosses of Tanner and Justin, and as matter of fact, neither of them, or Katie for that matter, are in that country, as we originally thought. This is… bigger than that." This surprised the group, but Dan was still confused. He didn't see how that was urgent.

"Okay, is there anything significant about that information that we're missing?" Trevor, who seemed to be thinking the same thing as Dan, asked the holograph. Professor, still fidgeting, answered while trying to adjust his glasses.

"Yes, well, this means that wherever Tanner and Justin are, they could be monitoring you at this very second."

"If they knew we were on the way to Brazil, wouldn't they have already tried to stop us?" Dan thought out loud, and Annie responded for the professor.

"That's what we're worried about. We think they might try to attack you while in the air. We're not sure what with, but we were just saying to be on the lookout and—" before Annie could finish, Marv's loud squawk startled everyone.

"Incoming… whatever that is!" Marv screeched, and the group looked forward to see three pitch black missile-shaped objects hurtling towards the griffin. The holograph buzzed and ended abruptly, while Dan ran over to Marv's head.

"Dive low, Marv!" The griffin nodded and maneuvered his wings to swoop lower. The missiles sailed overhead, Marv having successfully dodged the imminent danger. The group sighed in relief, but Gwen's worried face was unchanged.

"Guys, I think they're still coming after us," she pointed out that the missiles were still on our trail and had only taken a few extra seconds to track Marv again. The griffin grunted.

"Hold on to your feathers," the griffin yelled, and the group held on tight as Marv accelerated his speed, whizzing through the air. Emily screamed as the wind slapped violently around them. Marv swerved back and forth, making loops and rushing through clouds, but nothing veered the missiles off course. Marv flew straight at a normal pace then, and the missiles closed in.

"Marv… what are you doing?" Dan yelled, and suddenly, Marv shot straight down, causing everyone to scream in fear. Inches from the ocean, Marv turned back forward and skimmed the water.

"Did we lose them?" Marv asked. Dan turned around. The missiles were still in sight, but farther than before.

THE LOST JEWEL

"They're farther away, but it looks like they're still on our trail," he replied, brows furrowed in stress.

"Dan, I'm going to do something a little risky, but it should get the missiles off our course," Marv explained, and Dan nodded his agreement; he trusted the griffin with his life. Marv began a steady incline towards their previous altitude, and the missiles followed suit, not missing a beat. Gwen whimpered, looking back as the missiles closed in on them.

"Marv, are you sure you know what you're doing?" Trevor questioned, scratching his hair nervously.

"Marv!" Dan yelled, and the rest of the group looked over at him.

"What is it, my boy?" the griffin said.

"The missiles, they look… like they're charging something!" This caused everyone to look back at the flying weapons, and sure enough, there was a white glow glimmering around both missiles.

"What does that mean, Dan?" Emily yelled, the air making it hard to hear anything.

"I don't know!" Dan called back, watching the missiles intently. In a split second, the missiles shot forward at a speed twice as fast as before, and before Dan could even scream, both landed on the griffin's wings, causing Marv to screech in pain and spiral downward, falling so fast that it was all the group could do not to fall off his back.

"Hold on!" Dan tried to yell, but the fast-moving winds around him made it almost impossible for anything to be heard, and he closed his eyes a second before they impacted on the earth.

"Sir, the missiles were a success. Our calculations determined the group to have fallen on a deserted island in the South Atlantic Ocean."

"Perfect. Thank you, Katie," Justin dismissed the woman. He rolled his chair over to Tanner, who was looking at a computer screen.

"You hear that, my friend? Dan and his pesky friends are stuck on an island with an injured, if not dead, means of transportation," Justin chuckled evilly, patting Tanner on the back. No response. Justin raised an eyebrow.

"Something wrong, Tanner?"

Tanner was still silent, and Justin got up to look at what Tanner was observing on the screen. Showcased was a scene in the palace King Zala was currently in. The king himself was shown ripping his hair out and cursing multiple times as guards around him scrambled back and forth to heed to his needs.

"What a crazy way to work," Justin commented, but Tanner shook his head.

"No, Justin. Something happened to cause old Zala to erupt like that."

"Oh?" Justin asked.

THE LOST JEWEL

"Let me guess," Justin nudged Tanner. Even in their darkest moments, Justin couldn't help but crack a joke. Tanner wasn't fazed by this, which is how Justin knew this was serious.

"Before you do, let me tell you. Kris has escaped, most likely with Alissa, and the jewel," Tanner retorted angrily. The smile disappeared from Justin's face.

"How did this happen?" Tanner got up and slowly walked toward a window. The room was pitch black, much like the palace, with only two windows in the entire building. The tables were decked out in technological gear and a gigantic screen showcasing the world's happenings was centered in the front of the room.

"According to a report from Bailey, we think Kris guided Alissa and another, smaller companion to help him escape. The three of them are now in the jungle. Their exact whereabouts are currently unknown." Justin was still next to the screen Tanner was watching before, and looked down to see King Zala ordering his subjects around in a violent manner, pushing them back and forth and wrecking furniture around him in the process.

"King Zala has issued a full-on search for the trio, but based on previous results, that might not work." Tanner looked over at Justin, who was now in his own train of thought.

"What are you thinking?" Tanner asked him.

"If the search doesn't work out, I think I know what we might have to do to help Zala acquire them, and the jewel." Tanner immediately understood what Justin was referencing, nodding his head.

"That would be a logical course of action, only one problem—King Zala has demanded we not offer him any assistance what so ever when dealing with Alissa." Justin could not help but laugh at this.

"And how far has that gotten us, Tanner?" Both of them knew what had to be done.

"In any case, sooner or later King Zala is going to slip up in a way that can't be fixed. And I don't want to have to clean that mess up." Justin continued. Tanner agreed, scratching his 5'o clock shadow. Both of them walked over to the screen they had been previously watching, and sighed, shaking their heads.

"How did we find someone this crazy?" Justin asked of King Zala, who was now plopped on the floor, smashing the floor with his fists.

"I have no idea."

THE LOST JEWEL

CHAPTER 4: Uncharted Territory

    Lela sat in her room, wiping the tears from her face. There was nothing she could do. Her mother was crying constantly in her room and barely got a hold of herself enough to feed Lela. Her father was locked up in the dictator's prison, and her beloved sister Alissa was somewhere in the very same jungle that her elders told her to avoid at all costs. It was all she could do not to cry all day like her mother. Lela was stronger than that, though, and eventually, something came across her mind.

    Before she left, Lela looked through her covers until she found the lucky bracelet Alissa had gifted her on her birthday. She put it on, and proceeded to sneak out of the window. Once she was out, she began to sprint towards Zala's castle. As she ran, villagers around her looked and pointed, whispering to their friends,

"Oh, look. It's that poor girl. Her family's in shambles. What a sad soul." Lela sniffed, forcing herself to stay focused and not cry, and ran on, ignoring her friends that called to her as she passed by the school. She ignored the merchants yelling out as she darted by them. She covered her ears with her hands forcefully. In what seemed like forever, she reached the dictator's palace. She scurried to the side and hid behind the foliage that surrounded the building. She popped her head out through the bush she was inside to scope the scene. She could see guards marching out the back door into the jungle, probably in search of her sister. Once the entirety of them cleared out from the hallway, Lela quickly opened the nearest window and crawled in. Hearing more footsteps, she dashed into the closest room, and sighed in relief when it was only a side closet, full of old weapons and cleaning tools. She kept herself as still as possible to make sure she couldn't be seen as the guards walked by. It seemed like forever, but finally the last of the guards left and shortly after the corridor cleared, the door leading to the jungle was closed shut. The hall was empty, and no more guards were in Lela's sight. Slowly, she made her way out of the closet and tiptoed down the hallway in the opposite direction of the back door, making sure to continuously be on the lookout for any guards or servants of the king. Every minute or so she turned around to see if anyone was following her. Her father's voice rang in her head, *you can never be too safe*. She reached the corner and saw who she believed to be the king's assistant running back and forth in another corridor, crying. An eyebrow raised, she hid behind a plant and observed as he whimpered, tripping over himself as he ran down a set of stairs. Lela followed, making sure not to make too much noise. As soon as she reached the bottom of the stairs, she darted behind another plant. The assistant was in a corner mumbling at himself, and in the other side of the room was…

"Papa!" Her hand came over her mouth, but not fast enough, and the king's assistant looked up, instantly curious.

"Vajra, did you hear something?" Trying not to release the flow of tears that were about to a minute ago, Vajra shook his head.

"Must be my imagination. I'm going to get something to eat." As he walked into the kitchen, Lela ran up to the jail cell and looked up at her father with wet eyes.

"My girl… You must not stay here. You must go where it is safe." Vajra scolded her in a hushed tone, anxiously glancing back at the kitchen.

"I can't, papa! I can't without you!" Lela cried. Vajra's face looked grim but firm,

"Lela, you can. You're the strongest girl in this family, and you must act like it." Doubt streamed through

Lela's mind, but she nodded slowly. Vajra managed a weak smile, and held out his hand. Lela reached hers out as well, and for a moment, the bitter sweet company they shared was enough. A second later, however, and Lela couldn't stand it. She grabbed his hand through the cell bars and hugged it as strongly as she could.

"I love you," she mumbled in between sniffles, and without another word tip-toed back up the stairs. The king's assistant returned to the room just as the girl was out of sight, and smiled.

"Well, I have good news." Vajra raised an eyebrow, wiping off his wet face. Moop was too oblivious to notice the change in Vajra's demeanor, however.

"What's that, Moop?"

"I don't think King Zala is going to kill me!"

It was nice having someone else that wasn't an animal. That was what Alissa thought to herself as she, Kris, And Jo sat in a clearing deep in the jungle, miles away from the hideout. Jo had gathered a plethora of berries to feast on, and Kris had some cheese and bread in his pack. The three of them ate, while Alissa peppered Kris with questions.

"So you're saying you aren't from around here?"

"No, no. I come from America." Kris bit down on a bright red fruit and the juice spurted onto Alissa's face. Both of them laughed as Jo scampered over to lick it off her cheek.

THE LOST JEWEL

"I was a secret agent working for The Factory," Kris explained, and Alissa, tilted her head, confused.

"The Factory? Is this a special factory?" Kris nodded.

"It's basically a bunch of good people in a factory with magical powers," he stopped to take another bite, this time shielding the juices from Alissa. Her face remained curious, so Kris went on.

"We use these magical powers to write special books and give them to people. That's the simplest way I can put it. That's sort of like our cover-up job, though. Mainly we help keep the world's evil organizations at bay."

"And that is King Zala?" Alissa asked, wide-eyed. Kris spit the seed of the fruit he was eating to the side.

"If that is the dictator of your village, then yes, he is one of them." After a chunk of bread was downed, he kept talking.

"It may surprise you, but King Zala is not the commander of their organization."

"What?!" Alissa exclaimed. Kris shook his head, frowning. The bread crumbs were attracting ants, which Jo happily munched on, keeping them away from Alissa and Kris.

"Yeah, he's almost on the same level as his own henchmen in fact." Alissa was blown away. She didn't say anything.

"And these superiors he's got... They aren't bigger, or stronger. They're smarter and they have a *lot* more weapons." Alissa trembled. She could barely keep up with King Zala, but someone even more powerful? She closed her eyes tightly, trying to get the thought out of her mind. Kris put a hand on her shoulder.

"Hey, it's okay. We stopped them once, we can do it again!" Alissa looked up.

"You stopped them before?" Kris put the bread back in his pack and zipped it up, leaning on a tree and massaging the various mosquito bites crowding his skin.

"A few months ago, we set out to find Dan's parents. They were being held captive by the same organization that King Zala works for." Jo sat atop Alissa's shoulder, listening intently.

"Who is Dan?" Alissa asked. Kris stopped for a moment, and his eyes began to tear up. Wiping them away hastily, he responded.

"He's... a really good friend. Anyway, we found his parents after going a long journey, but I was captured at the last second by the leaders, Tanner and Justin, and one of their workers Katie." Alissa stopped chewing on her berry.

"So these leaders, Tanner and Justin... Where are they now?"

"We don't know. After I was captured I was stripped of all my gadgets and all ways of communication. I managed to salvage some of them when I was being shipped to Brazil.

I had no way of figuring out where in the world I was though." Alissa nodded slowly. Jo scratched his head.

"Chi chi?" Alissa translated for him, as all Kris could do was shrug.

"I think he wants to know why you became an agent." Kris wiped his brow and pushed his fingers through his hair, taking his time before answering.

"Well I… never knew my parents. I was born in The Factory's main headquarters and for as long as I've been alive, my twin and I have been under the professor's care.

"He took us through intensive training to become agents, and from that point on, that was our life. I don't know much else," Kris finished, wiping a tear away from his eyes. Jo squeaked, and before Kris could ask, Alissa told him.

"I think he just said you're very emotional." Kris laughed and brought his pack out from behind him again, unzipping it and sorting through the devices inside. He pulled out a broken rectangular screen with a silver outline and an antennae on the top. Jo crawled down from Alissa's shoulder to look it over, poking at the blank black screen.

"This was a communicator; what we use to talk to The Factory workers when we're away from home." Dan turned it over to reveal some writing. Alissa's forehead creased in stress.

"Do you not read?" Blushing, Alissa shook her head. Kris smiled.

"It's fine. It says 'The Factory'!" Jo shoved his tiny fingers in the concaves that the letters created, and Kris pushed him away, chuckling.

"Tanner and Justin destroyed it while I was unconscious and I have no way of knowing where my sister, or anyone, is." Alissa frowned, and Jo did as well.

"So how long have you been stuck in that jail cell?" Alissa said, feeling the communicator in her hands. Kris sighed, scratching his head. Even though he was making an effort to answer her questions enthusiastically, she could tell he was extremely fatigued.

"It's been a really long time, that's all I know. Eating the same vomit soup and stale crackers every day three times a day does get old." Kris shook his head.

"What was the question again?" He mumbled. Alissa put an arm around him.

"Why don't we get some rest? It is getting late," she said soothingly, and Kris agreed, yawning.

"We need our energy to keep escaping from those bad guys," Kris muttered before knocking out against the tree. Jo crawled in front of him, snuggling up and squeaking happily. Alissa leaned back as well, smiling at Jo.

"We're almost like a family!" She joked, and Jo chirped in response. Soon, Jo was asleep too, and Alissa was left alone with her thoughts and the dark, looming jungle that surrounded her. The leaves seemed to shine off the moon and reflect into Alissa's eyes, making her even sleepier. As her eyes became heavier and heavier, she looked into the sky, imagining her father, mother, and sister, smiling at her. Lela's bright, cheerful face made Alissa warm inside. She finally closed her eyes, and all of sudden, watched in horror as her father was taken from her mother and sister. Two guards came running in to the blank space, both of them with the faces of demons, yelling in an unknown language. Their eyes were bright yellow and sticking out of their hats were devil horns. They grabbed Vajra by the arms harshly and carried him out. Alissa's mother screamed at the top of her lungs and Lela sat on the floor, speechless. The tears began to flow until Alissa couldn't hold them anymore. Like something inside her had changed—she couldn't explain it, but as she watched her father get ripped from her family's life, and her mother lose her grip on reality, she began to fall deeper and deeper, until Alissa could see Lela's eyes turn completely black. Alissa ran over to her and her mother, but they couldn't see her, or feel her. Alissa watched hopelessly as her mother crumbled by Lela's side, hugging her tightly and sobbing crazily. Alissa began to cry as well. A black hole appeared under her family and sucked them in in a split second, leaving her all alone in a vast pitch black abyss. She reached out in absolute shock, but no one was there anymore, and her hand remained empty. Alissa laid out on the ground, covering her face with her hands. Nothing she could do could make the image of her helpless, broken parents disappear.

THE LOST JEWEL

Dan was the first to come to, rubbing his eyes forcefully. He rose from the ground slowly, yawning as he did. He felt like something was burning, and looked down sluggishly to see sand underneath his feet. His brain then realized the sand was burning hot. Letting out a scream, Dan dashed for the ocean. As soon as set his feet in the water, he sighed gratefully. Ocean? He blinked again, confused. Where was he? He turned around to look behind him. There was a small cape of beach where he and his friends had landed, but the rest of this island was completely covered in thick foliage. He couldn't make out any sign of civilization. Cautiously, he took a step out of the ocean and onto the sand, but now that his feet were wet it didn't hurt. He walked over to Marv to examine the damage. Both his wings were charred and dried blood covered most of his skin. Dan couldn't bear to look at the wound for much longer and quickly trudged over to where Trevor had landed to wake him. Dan poked the side of his body. Trevor's light brown hair was almost completely covering his eyes and both his hands were scarred with cuts and minor wounds. He slowly awoke, mumbling and grumbling until he noticed Dan next to him.

"What happened?" He groaned, stretching his limbs out. Dan shrugged. He couldn't quite remember himself. In a few seconds, the pain from the burning hot sand came into Trevor's senses and he yelled, jumping up and down. Dan pointed to the ocean and Trevor sprinted for it, sliding into the cold water and sighing deeply. Dan went over to wake up Gwen and Emily, who were near each other, close to Marv's beak. They both woke and before they could even feel the pain, Dan suggested they go to the ocean to cool off their feet. They nodded, a little fazed, and headed over to where Trevor was. Dan hurried back over to Marv, who was now somewhat conscious. Dan put his hand on the griffin's back, stroking it comfortingly. The bird cawed weakly.

"My friend…" Marv coughed, his beak filled with sand. Dan watched solemnly as he spit out the stuff and continued.

"I do not think I will be able to take flight any time soon." Dan nodded. He didn't expect much else. Dan sat next to Marv's head and managed a smile, patting the griffin's back.

"It's alright, Marv. This place isn't so bad! At least we didn't get stranded… Uh, somewhere else," he said, scratching his head. Marv chuckled, and his eyes began to flutter.

"Dan, my boy, I'm going to have a nap. I…" the fatigue hit him before he could finish, and in seconds Marv was knocked out. Dan slowly made his way over to where his friends were, near the ocean. He laid down next to them and interrupted their chatter.

"Any idea where we are, guys?" Dan asked. Gwen shrugged immediately and Emily gave him a look.

"We're just as clueless as you are," Trevor answered, cracking his knuckles absentmindedly. Dan's forehead creased and Gwen shoved him.

"Hey, dumbo! What about the communicator?" Gwen exclaimed. Dan jumped up. *The communicator!*

"Thanks, Gwen!" He yelled, and darted back over to where they had initially landed. He searched back and forth for the device, running in circles around Marv, but there was no sight of the contraption.

"It must have fell off into the ocean when we were hit," Dan called, sounding defeated as he walked back over to the beach's end. The four of them sat, looking out at the horizon. All they could see was ocean, shimmering under the glistening sun.

"There's nothing out there. I can't even see another island," Emily remarked, shielding her eyes from the blazing light.

"Well, I hate to be the bearer of bad news, but we don't have anything to eat. We're going to have to find food somehow." Trevor turned around and the rest of them did as well, looking at the greenery that surrounded the small piece of beach they were situated on. The trees loomed high above the rest of the plants, their huge leaves making an umbrella-shaped top to the thin, rustic-brown trunks. Some shorter tropical trees surrounded the bigger ones, and they littered the rest of the jungle area. Tons of large shrubs sprouted from the ground, each with huge leaves and roots with sharp, jagged shapes. The grass growing off the jungle floor looked to be tall as well, reaching to about Gwen's knees. Dan spotted a group of brightly colored birds sitting atop a family of shrubs and leaves near the edge of the forest, munching on some kind of worm. To the right of them, a gigantic caterpillar creature with a purple body and light brown hair covering its skin crawled on a tree trunk.

"It's so fat!" Gwen giggled, pointed out the critter to her friends, and they all gasped as a huge sky-blue bird that none of them had seen before swooped down and snatched the bug into its mouth. As the winged beast flew away, Trevor gulped.

"I don't think this island is very safe," he said. Emily and Gwen agreed. Dan remained speechless, staring at the birds.

"We should probably stay on the beach. It seems like those animals don't like the sand," Emily commented, nervously fixing her brown hair. The group mumbled agreement.

"We can make an SOS in the beach!" Gwen suggested, clapping her hands. Dan, still silent, slowly shook his head.

"Dan?" Emily called. He had wandered away from the group and was sitting by the shore. She came over and sat in front of him. Her murky hazel eyes looked into Dan's.

"Dan, what's wrong?"

"I don't think we'll be alive long enough for our SOS to be seen." Silence. "What I mean is, we are in a very bad place." After a couple more minutes of silence, Dan got up, dusted himself off, and walked back to where Trevor and Gwen were. Emily followed suit. Dan cleared his throat.

"Guys, Trevor is right."

"So what you're saying is—"

"Yeah, Gwen, there's no getting around it. We have to find food inside the jungle." The four of them didn't speak. The thought scared all of them, but the logic behind Dan's words were hard to ignore.

"You're right, Dan," Emily said grudgingly, and Gwen whimpered.

"I'll just stay on this nice beach and wait for you guys, okay?" Gwen whimpered. Dan looked at Gwen's big eyes, and put his hands on her shoulders. It was his turn to look into her eyes.

"Gwen, you're a brave girl. We need your help. If we can gather enough food to keep us alive until Marv heals, we won't have to go into the jungle again, okay?" After a minute, Gwen nodded, sniffling. Dan smiled and patted her back. He got up and the rest of them followed.

"First, we're going to have to create some container to store water," Trevor said, and Dan agreed. Emily walked over to a plant with particularly large leaves and picked one off. To her surprise, the leaf immediately shriveled into a crumpled brown ball. She plopped it on the ground and looked back at the rest of the group.

"This plant won't work," she commented, shaking her head. Soon enough, Dan found another plant with big leaves that held up when picked off and was responsive to the water. The group walked back over to the shore with a handful of the same plant and Gwen showed the group how to tie the plants into a shape that could hold water.

"Where'd you learn this from, Gwen?" Dan asked after she helped him finish his personal leaf container.

"Secret Agent training of course!" She exclaimed, and Dan laughed. With all her childish actions, he had completely forgotten the girl was an expertly trained spy. Once they each had a leaf container readily filled with water, Dan took one to Marv and carefully roused the griffin from his sleep. The bird yawned and stretched his talons out.

"Marv, we've got some water for you," he said softly. The griffin nodded, opening his beak. Dan slowly poured the water until the container was empty. Marv uttered a weak thank you, closed his eyes, and drifted back into slumber. Dan went back over to the others, who were closer to the water, to come up with a plan.

"Here's what I'm thinking. We go in as a group, and Gwen will figure out which foods are poisonous and which aren't, thanks to her training. We'll take another one of those leaves to hold it all, and as soon as we think we have enough to last us, we'll come back to the beach. No wandering and no exploring," Dan explained. The rest of them nodded in agreement. After a deep breath, Dan spoke again.

"Then let's go." With that, the four of them took their feet out of the cold water and began their trek, entering the jungle a few feet away from where the gigantic leaf plant was. Instantly, the group could feel a difference in climate. The air was moist and humid, sticking to their skin and making it harder to breath. The tall grass at the jungle floor made their ankles itch annoyingly, and bugs buzzed continuously throughout the jungle, flying around their heads. Trevor reached out to snatch one, but they were all too fast for him, and Dan comforted him, trying to crack a joke.

"Hey, it would be great to have some bug spray right now wouldn't it?" Trevor just shook his head, obviously not in the mood. The trees above had huge canopies, shielding them from the deadly sun and making the atmosphere inside the jungle much cooler. Dan could only imagine how it would feel *without* the canopy. There were flamboyant plants all over the jungle; bright yellow, red, pink, and orange flowers, you name it. It was a rainbow of foliage. He could already feel the insects attempting to bite at his skin and slapped his legs every minute that passed. Angrily, he surveyed his friends, who were having the same problem.

"Does anyone know where exactly we're going?" Trevor said. Nobody had an answer for him.

THE LOST JEWEL

"We're not really going anywhere. Just keep going straight and keep on the lookout for food," Dan said, and with a shrug, Trevor continued on. Dan felt like every time he stopped moving, hundreds of pests immediately flew over and began biting at his body. He watched Gwen and Emily do the same, both of them scratching violently at their legs and arms.

"We really need something to keep these bugs away," Emily grunted, slapping her knee to kill a mosquito.

"That would be nice, but we have no bug spray in the jungle, Em, that was a joke earlier," Dan commented sarcastically. Gwen shook her head.

"There's some plants that bugs don't like. Just look around for one that doesn't have any near it and we'll rub the leaves of it on our skin." It wasn't an easy plan, but it was a plan nonetheless, and so Dan forced himself to look around for any plants that were obviously disliked by the bugs. Unfortunately, it seemed like there were none around. Gwen took off her head band and began swatting at the insects, swishing the cloth violently to keep them away.

"Trevor, can I use your glasses for something?" Gwen asked, a peculiar smile appearing on her face. Bewildered, Trevor shook his head.

"Why would you need my glasses?" Gwen shrugged mysteriously. Trevor shuddered and looked over at Dan, who seemed amused.

"I think she has a serious problem," he whispered to his friend. Dan chuckled.

"Maybe you don't need to be so uptight. It looks like we'll be here a while, so you better get used to this," Dan said in an attempt to lighten up his friend, and Trevor nodded, adjusting his glasses. Emily seemed the least optimistic, her face bright red with anger. For some reason, the bugs had focused on her the most, and she was already bitten in several places.

"We should probably find something quick," Trevor exclaimed, noticing Emily's torrid facial expression. He laughed for a moment, but a dark glance from Emily shut him up quickly.

"Gwen, you see anything?" Dan asked, surveying his surroundings after every step.

"No, I feel like there's just a bunch of the same plants, no variety," Gwen mumbled, deep in focus with the foliage around her.

"Is that abnormal or something?" Trevor questioned, and Gwen nodded.

"Especially in a tropical island like this. Usually there's thousands of plant species for every square inch," Gwen explained, turning over a leaf and sniffing another flower. Emily yelped, as she had scratched a bug bite so forcefully it began to ooze a clear blue liquid.

"What is this?!" Emily retorted, and Gwen quickly used her headband to clean up the wound.

"Looks like pus to me," Gwen said seriously, and Emily gasped, disgusted. Gwen gave her a questioning look. She angrily shook her head, sticking her tongue out.

"I just… That word is repulsive!" Emily stammered, embarrassed. Gwen simply giggled, and before Dan could notice her mischievous smirk, she began.

"What, pus?" She smiled, crunching leaves as they walked, picking out the loudest ones to annoy Emily.

"Yes! Ew!" Emily exclaimed, trying to wipe the oozing liquid on her shirt, which was already covered in dirt and sand. Gwen began hopping as they walked through the jungle, chanting 'pus' in a maniacal matter.

"Pus pus pus pus!" Gwen sang mockingly, sticking her tongue at Emily. Trevor noticed Emily's fists; she was clenching them harder every time Gwen repeated the word. Trevor grabbed Emily, who was shaking from irritation, and steadied her with his arms.

"Whoa there, calm down," He said soothingly, and Emily sighed, nodding. She, somewhat reluctantly, apologized to Gwen.

"Sorry I almost blew up on you," she muttered, absentmindedly scratching a bite. Gwen looked hurt at first, but then grinned and clapped her hands.

"That's okay, I got you two lovebirds to cuddle!" She giggled, and Trevor and Emily both blushed, but neither of them looked like they regretted it. Dan chuckled, pushing Gwen playfully.

"Come on now, let's keep looking for the things we need," he directed the group's attention back to the task at hand, but as Gwen continued to purposefully jump on every dead leaf in sight, Dan noticed Trevor holding Emily's hand. He thought back to his life back at The Factory. He wondered how Peter and Annie were doing. Knowing them, they were probably worried about the group. Dan thought about Kris, probably somewhere alone in Brazil, possibly being tortured because of their carelessness. His heart panged with pain, and he blinked hard. He had to keep looking for plants. He turned his focus back to the greenery around him and frowned. He felt like he had seen the exact same cluster of plants five minutes ago. He kept looking around as they walked, confusion continuing to build. That vine, this plant, those trees, they all seemed so oddly familiar. It was a jungle, that's probably just imagination, Dan thought to himself, but then he realized something. Quickly, he looked at Gwen who was hopping on the dead leaves, just as she had five minutes ago. Dan stopped abruptly, and the rest of the group followed his lead, halting themselves.

"Something up, Dan?" Trevor asked, but Dan didn't say anything. He knelt down and picked the leaves around his feet up quickly and began to run backwards. Confused, the others reluctantly followed him.

"Hey, what are you doing?" Emily called after Dan, but nothing could stop him. He began to sprint, sweat dripping from his hair, his eyes blinking rapidly. He couldn't comprehend it. What was going on? He stopped as he saw the cluster of plants that he had remembered, and looked down at the ground. Just as he had thought. Finally the rest of the group caught up to him, and Trevor complained, panting.

"What the heck?" Dan put up a hand, signaling him to hold on, and pointed to the ground.

"Gwen... didn't you crush these five minutes ago?" Suddenly curious, the three pushed Dan aside to see what he had discovered. In the exact same place as before lay the dry leaves that Gwen had crushed. Bewildered, Gwen picked one up, and before Dan could say anything, crushed it in her hand. They waited a moment. The remains of the leaf stayed on the ground and no new leaf had spurted from the ground. Puzzled, Dan shook his head.

"Then how did this happen? I don't understand!" He put his hands over his face, his brain become crowded with thought as he tried to make sense of the situation. Trevor and Emily frowned, concerned of Dan's behavior.

"The jungle's really getting to him," Gwen mumbled to the two.

"Don't be silly!" An unknown voice chirped. The group, startled, jumped up. They quickly glanced around, but no one was in sight.

"Who said that?!" Emily called.

"Up here!" They looked up to see a brightly colored bird smiling down at them. The bird's wings were a bright green and its body was a light shade of pink. Squawking with its shining yellow beak, it exclaimed,

"Surprised that I can talk? All joybirds can!" The group's blank faces made the bird smirk.

"Joybirds are native to this island. That's why you've never heard of them." Dan raised a finger, his face wild.

"The… the bird is talking," Dan said, sounding like a lunatic. The bird, now annoyed, flew down from her perch on the tree above them and conked Dan's cranium.

"Tell me something I don't know, bub!" The bird exclaimed, resting on Gwen's head. Giggling, Gwen reached out for it and the bird softly touched her hand with its wing.

"Who are you?" Gwen asked, and the bird flew over to Emily, who seemed frozen in shock.

"The name's Walter, but you can call me Walt!" He chirped, and glided over to Trevor. Swiftly taking the glasses of his face, Walt put them on mockingly and Gwen laughed, applauding. Dan, still a little baffled, tried to calm Gwen down.

"So…" He started, but Walt seemed to be one step ahead of him.

"You're in a time loop. They're very common here!" Walt continued to fly to and fro, now munching on a blue leaf next to Trevor.

THE LOST JEWEL

"Where is here?" Emily asked. The bird flew over to her and snapped his beak on her hair, causing Emily to scream. Squawking in delight, the bird flew over to another tree and landed, looking down at the group with tired eyes.

"You're stranded on the Lagoon Island, my friends!" Walt swooped down and sat on the jungle floor.

"No one's ever heard of it because the island itself is in its own time loop." Walt stopped and flew over to the blue plant and began eating again. "Getting stranded here is a pretty grand accomplishment."

"What do you mean?" Trevor muttered.

"You basically have to be in the exact coordinates at the exact timing for the island to even appear," the bird explained, returning Trevor's glasses.

"Our luck, of course!" Trevor exclaimed angrily, turning around and walking off. Walt chirped, confused.

"What's up with him?"

"He's always a little uptight, cut him some slack," Dan explained, watching Walt closely as he flew to a third tree, now forming a complete circle around the group. The bird never seemed to stop moving, always chomping its beak and swooping from place to place. *Sort of like the island,* he thought to himself.

"So explain to us what a time loop is," Dan prompted. Walt glided over to Gwen, who had become infatuated with the plump pink bird the moment she laid eyes on it. Accepting Walt into her arms, he responded.

"Basically, you four have been walking in the same area multiple times. As soon as you get to the edge of a time loop, it resets and you begin again. It makes you believe you've been walking in circles." Horrified, Trevor's jaw dropped.

"How do we get out of it?!" He yelled. The bird squawked in a way that sounded like laughter, flapping his wings into Trevor's face.

"I know how to get you out, don't worry!" Walt flew over to a nearby tree, and Gwen stood up, raising an eyebrow.

"Will you help us?" Walt finally stopped moving around and sat, frozen. He looked to be mulling over his options. Dan didn't take his eyes off the bird for a second. Finally, the bird glided down to Gwen's head and chirped.

"I guess I'll lend you guys a hand." Relieved, Emily sighed and Dan wiped the sweat off his forehead. He looked around the jungle, taking note of all the plants they had seen before.

"What do we do first?" He asked Walt, who chuckled.

"Nothing, only us joybirds can get people out of time loops. The animals of this island aren't affected by them," he explained. "Follow me!" Walt took off in the direction that the group had previously been going. Gwen darted after him first, leaving the others hurrying to keep up with the two.

"Gwen, keep him in your sights!" Dan called after her, already exhausted. Trevor and Emily were running as well, and in a few minutes, they had caught up to Gwen and Walt. Dan looked around.

"This is where we were when I realized something was wrong," He noted, and Walt nodded. He flew in front of the group and a few feet ahead of where Dan had his breakdown.

"This is the edge of the time loop you were in," Walt explained to Dan.

"It looks exactly the same as the rest of the jungle, how can you tell?" Trevor questioned, and Walt shrugged.

"All animals can see time loop borders. Humans can't. Simple, no?" Trevor grumbled, and Gwen pointed to the outside.

"So how do we get out of it? Come on Walt!" Gwen asked impatiently. Walt squawked, hovering above the four.

"Be patient!" He then turned his beak to where he had said the edge of the time loop was, and opened his beak slowly. He flapped into the air, holding out his wings, as if he was holding something up. To Dan, it looked as if it was a pain for the bird, who was exerting enough pressure that his body was shaking.

"Walk right under me, no more than three or four steps," Walt grunted, and the group nodded, walking through the invisible opening Walt had created one by one. Once

Emily had walked out, Walt shot forward, smashing into a tree. Gwen laughed as Emily ran over to pick him up.

"That's the worst part," the bird muttered, dusting off his wings. Dan went over to Walt and Emily, patting the birds head.

"Thanks for helping us out, Walt," he smiled at the bird.

"Don't mention it. Also, to keep those bugs away…" He flew over to the blue plant he had been munching on before.

"Chew on these and you should be okay." Dan took the mound of leaves Walt was carrying and expressed his gratitude. Emily hadn't looked more elated since they landed on the island.

"Walt, one more question…" Trevor started.

"What's that, nerd?" Walt chirped, resting on Gwen's head again. Trevor scratched his head nervously.

"Has anyone ever… been rescued once they get stranded here?" A bout of silence. The bird, for all his wit, was suddenly hesitant to say anything. A feeling of despair fell upon the group as they realized what the colorful creature's silence meant. Walt plucked a feather off of his left wing and handed it to Trevor, who reluctantly took it.

"If you all are the first ones, have this is a reminder of me. Good luck… You'll need it."

CHAPTER 5: Stranded

"That bird was nice!" Gwen exclaimed, skipping around a bush.

"He could've told us how to make sure not to get into another time loop," Trevor grumbled angrily. Emily put a hand on his shoulder.

"Are you still angry about his nerd comment?" Emily asked softly. His face bright red, Trevor turned away from Emily, who only sighed and forced him to look at her.

"You're not a nerd, don't worry," Emily tried to soothe him, smiling. After a few minutes of unresponsiveness, Trevor shrugged and adjusted his glasses.

"So what do we do now?" He asked Dan. Dan was busy picking a yellow fruit off of a plant nearby. It was about the size of Gwen's fist.

"Gwen, is this edible?" Dan asked hopefully, handing it over to her. She rolled it over in her hands, squeezing it gently and then sniffing its surface. She then threw the fruit back into the jungle.

"That would kill you in three seconds," she exclaimed, and the group groaned in unison.

"We're going to die if we don't find something," Trevor whined, tugging at his shirt. Emily nodded, chewing up a blue leaf. The humidity of the jungle was getting to them.

"Well I'm sorry, would you rather have me let you guys eat poisonous fruit?" Gwen snapped, and Dan calmed her down as Emily and Trevor scoffed. The trees were becoming so huge and thick that Dan could barely tell what time of day it was. Dan thought of something, observing the height of the tree trunks. He looked at Gwen, who seemed to be the most energetic out of the entire group. Poking her, he pointed to the top of one of the trees.

"Do you think you can climb that and look for anything helpful?" Dan asked.

"Sounds like fun!" Gwen agreed, and ran over to the trunk. Without hesitation she made her way up the tree, and after a few minutes she reached the highest branches, where the canopy began. Dan motioned for her to continue to the very top, and she did so, throwing her body through the wall of leaves.

"See anything?" He yelled out. A response came back but it was inaudible. The group waited for Gwen to come back down, and asked again.

"Was there anything?" Trevor said, and Gwen shook her head.

"I couldn't see any food, but I saw something interesting… It looked like a volcano or something. A big mountain." Emily raised an eyebrow.

"Well, was there food on it?" Emily impatiently asked. Gwen shrugged.

"I don't know, I couldn't get a good view of the summit, but maybe we should just head over that way." Seeing no other option, the group agreed and Gwen began to lead them in direction of the volcano. The jungle seemed to only get thicker and thicker, with the plants becoming bigger and the air feeling heavier. Multi-colored flowers and shrubbery littered the forest; the bright, flavorful colors made Dan and the rest of the group even hungrier. After glancing at a beige flower with a brown center, he began to imagine a giant, juicy hamburger in front of him. Dreamily, he reached out to take a bite, only to find himself bumping into Trevor.

"Hey, what gives?" Trevor snapped sharply. Dan, embarrassed and worried, confusedly shrugged his shoulders and mumbled an apology. He didn't know how much longer he could go on without food. Suddenly, Emily collapsed on the jungle floor, the cluster of blue leaves in her hand fluttering around her. Startled, Trevor and Dan hurried to her side.

"Emily, what's wrong?!" Gwen asked, worried. Emily coughed, scratching at her arm vigorously.

"Need… food…" She whispered weakly. The boys tried to help her to her feet, but she could barely stand. Dan realized what he had to do.

"Trevor… You stay here with Emily. Gwen and I need to find food. We're gonna sprint around this place, look under every nook and cranny… Once we feed her, we can keep going to the volcano and…" Dan trailed off. Trevor nodded, shooing them off.

"Yeah yeah, now go find some grub or else Emily won't be the only one fainting from starvation." Dan laughed a nervous laugh, and Gwen kissed Emily's cheek.

"We'll be back, Em!" She called as Emily groaned, still itching her bug bites. Dan and Gwen made their way through the jungle until they couldn't see Trevor and Emily anymore. He stopped and turned to Gwen.

"This is serious, Gwen. We need to find food. From this point on, there is no joking around. There is no—" before he could finish his speech, Gwen pointed at something with huge eyes.

"Food!" She exclaimed, dashing to Dan's right. Dan ran as fast as he could, trying to catch up to the speedy spy.

THE LOST JEWEL

When she wants to, she's light on her feet, Dan thought, huffing and puffing. Finally, Gwen stopped, and Dan tried to figure out what she saw. In front of them was a tiny plant in the middle of the ground with swirling pink polka-dots. Gwen sighed, rubbing her forehead.

"Sorry, I… thought it was…" Dan held up a hand, motioning for her to stop.

"I understand. Let's keep looking, okay?" She got up and they continued their search, looking under leaves and shoveling around bushes, hoping for something. The expedition went for hours. Every minute that went by, a new plant or fruit would appear in their sights and Gwen would inevitably mark it off as poisonous or deadly, causing Dan's stomach to grumble louder and louder. Soon, the food hallucinations were flowing in Dan's brain consistently; everywhere he looked there was a sundae, or a basket of French fries. Gwen was having the same problem, reaching out to scoop out ice cream from a non-existent tub. Dan wiped the sweat off his forehead for what seemed like the hundredth time today, and stopped for a moment, catching his breath. He called over to Gwen, who was inspecting a peculiar looking purple sprout.

"Anything?"

"Nope. Poisonous." She responded, throwing the sprout back on the ground and rubbing her stomach. They resumed their trek, absolutely desperate for something to occupy their mouths. They had almost run out of blue leaves, and Gwen reached for the second to last one before Dan grabbed her hand.

"We need those to keep the bugs away, remember?" Slowly, Gwen pulled her arm back and they continued, trying not to conjure up delicious meals in their head. Gwen trotted up to a large tree trunk, and slunk down to the floor in front of it, putting her hands to her face. Dan could clearly see the tears begin to fall. She sat there for a while as Dan awkwardly stood in front of her, muttering words of comfort. Dan completely understood her. They had lost their way, and seemed farther away from saving Kris than ever before. He knelt down next to Gwen, and put his arm on her shoulder. She looked up slowly, peering into his eyes.

"Dan?" She whimpered, before he could say anything himself.

"Yes, Gwen?"

"Marv... Is he gonna... Is he gonna make it?" This sentence hit Dan like a brick. He hadn't thought of it that way. He remembered how disgusted he had been by Marv's injury. He didn't take any time to inspect the severity, or investigate if Marv needed more attention.

"I can't answer that, Gwen. I just don't know," Dan replied, a stone cold expression on his face. Gwen nodded, wiping the tears off her cheeks. She stood up, and took Dan's hand, squeezing it hard.

"Well, we better find some food so at least Marv might." She stomped off, forcing Dan to follow suit, hand in hand. After a few minutes of walking, Dan began to notice something.

"Hey, Gwen, something's changed, don't you think?"

"Yeah, I noticed it too, but I don't know exactly what it is." For a moment, they were both silent as they walked. Dan stopped, and knelt down to a shrub of dark red leaves. He felt them in between his fingers, and exclaimed,

"They're wet! The plants are all moist!" Gwen released her hand from Dan's and ran over to a tree to feel its bark.

"You're right, they definitely are! Maybe that means something edible will show up around here!" Gwen said with hope. Dan gave her a thumbs up, and they trudged on with a bustling, newfound confidence. The leaves above completely blocked out the sky at this point in the jungle. Dan couldn't tell how late in the day it was, but he was aware they'd been in the jungle for several hours. The duo continued to follow the trail of moist greenery, and as they walked, the variety of plants continued to grow, with purple and yellow flowers to blue and red bushes. Dan felt he was in a jungle made of candy, except that all the candy he could see was poisonous. Gwen was a little farther ahead, and she stopped at the beginning of a small clearing.

"What's up, Gwen?" Dan asked, and Gwen motioned for him to come over.

THE LOST JEWEL

"You'll want to see this! Hurry!" Gwen called. Concerned that something might be wrong, Dan darted over to Gwen, but right before he reached her, his foot slipped from underneath him on the moist ground and he caused Gwen and himself to tumble down a pit that she had been standing before. Screaming, the two of them fell for what seemed like forever, with Gwen yelling incomprehensibly at Dan. Finally, they both landed on the ground with a loud thud. The room they had fallen into was pitch black, and neither of them could see anything. Dan grumbled, feeling around to make some understanding of his surroundings. The ground wasn't nearly as moist as the upper portion of the jungle was, and the ground was littered with dry leaves.

"Gwen?" He called. Her response was a shriek of pain, startling Dan.

"What is it?! Gwen!" He yelled, frantically crawling around, trying to find her.

"I'm fine, I just fell on something really hard, I think it was a rock…" Gwen muttered angrily. By the sound of her voice, she didn't sound too far away, so Dan was a little relieved. However, time was extremely important, and if they didn't get out soon, much worse things would happen to not only them, but Emily, and Marv.

"Gwen, we have to find a way out of here!" Dan exclaimed, trying to find the walls of this area he had fallen into.

THE LOST JEWEL

"That would make a lot of sense, yeah," Gwen sarcastically answered. They both rummaged around, without luck.

"Try to find a wall and follow it! Figure out if there's an entrance to wherever I am. I'll do the same," Dan said in an encouraging tone, although he didn't feel very hopeful himself. The leaves crunched loudly under Dan's hands and feet, filling his head. Suddenly, his fingers felt a new sensation—some sort of wall made out of compact soil.

"I found a wall!" Dan yelled to inform Gwen.

"I did too!" She responded. Dan began to crawl with one hand on the ground and the other on the wall, trying to shape out the room with his mind. Before doing so, he made an indention into the soil to mark where he had begun. Much to his disheartenment, he reached his indention after what seemed like seconds.

"There's no exit on this side," Dan called nervously, and no response came from Gwen. He scratched his hair for a bit, and then spoke again.

"Gwen?"

"One second, dumbo! I'm on to something!" That shut Dan up pretty quickly. After a few more moments of silence, Gwen yelled out to Dan.

"I'm going to try to dig a hole through the wall, because I think the rooms we're in are right up next to each other. You do that too, alright?" Dan nodded before he remembered Gwen couldn't see him.

"Yeah, I got it." They began to dig, and for a while it seemed that it was in vain. Suddenly, Dan felt the familiar feeling of human skin contact with his as he was digging. He smiled, and the two of them made the hole big enough so Gwen could climb through, but she didn't.

"Come on, Gwen!" Dan hurried her, but she remained put in her own room.

"If I go over there, it does nothing. We're still not going to know any way out of here." Gwen said sadly. Dan thought about it, and agreed.

"Hey, if we put our heads together we can definitely think of something!" Dan exclaimed. A light bulb went off in Gwen's head. Before Dan could do anything, she climbed through the hole, bumping into Dan as she entered his room.

"Hold onto my hand so I don't lose you in the dark," Dan said, grabbing hold of her left hand. She crawled around and began to push the soil on the other side of Dan downward as quickly as she could, moving with precision. After a while, she stopped and glanced over at Dan, who sat motionless, completely perplexed.

"Dan, don't just stand there dummy. Help me out here!" Dan shook his head to wake himself up and positioned himself next to Gwen, burrowing the same way she was. Soil began to break underneath the holes the two of them were making, causing the soil directly under their bodies to rise in level.

"It's almost like an elevator," Gwen giggled, obviously proud of her innovative thinking. Dan smiled, but continued to dig, not letting his focus waver. After what seemed like hours, the soil level had risen to a point where they could jump up to the ledge and crawl out, using every last ounce of energy they had left. Once both of them had gotten out of the hole, they plopped onto the forest floor and sighed, eyes closed.

"Dan, are your forearms on fire?"

"You bet, Gwen."

The two of them sat there, silently groaning in pain. The adrenaline Dan felt digging masked what was a daunting physical task, and it hit him hard once they made it out. It didn't take long for him to remember what they'd set out to do, though.

"Gwen, as much as I hate to say this, we need to keep looking for food," he grunted, willing himself to get off the ground. Gwen sighed and slid her arms up, pushing her tiny body to an upward position. She looked around, scanning the forestry for any sight of food. Dan attempted to look under some large leaves nearby as she analyzed the surroundings.

"On the bright side, these plants are still moist, so we might still be on the right track," Gwen pointed out.

"Alright, well, if we can't find the source of these moist plants, talking about it won't be much help," Dan huffed, tired and hungry. His stomach roared in despair, and Dan instinctively clutched it with both hands.

They walked a bit farther off from the hole they'd fallen in, and Gwen constantly let her finger graze the nearby foliage to affirm that they were still moist. Dan dragged along, seemingly weighed down by his immense fatigue.

"Dan, this is it!!" Gwen shrieked in excitement, zipping to her right, where a bushel of bright orange speckled berries stood. Dan mustered a half-hearted thumbs up, and Gwen hurriedly stuffed all of the berries from the shrub into a bag, handing Dan a couple as well.

"You can eat them, they aren't poisonous. We hit the jackpot!" Gwen clamored happily, almost immediately skipping back in the direction of Emily and Trevor. Dan followed suit, feeling rejuvenated by the food they'd discovered. Before long, they came across Emily lying quietly on the ground, and Trevor squatting next to her, fanning her face with an enormous leaf.

"You found something?" Trevor inquired, and Gwen nodded, giddy with joy. Trevor clapped his hands and woke Emily up, who looked even worse than when Dan and Gwen left. There were bags under her eyes, and her skin was clammy and pale. Gwen grabbed her hand, manually opened it, and laid a large handful of berries inside.

"Em, these are for you," Gwen explained, helping her sit up. Emily slowly opened her mouth and let the berries fall down her throat, chomping down on them at the pace of a sloth. Almost instantaneously, color began to come back to Emily's face as she swallowed.

"Can I have some more?!" She croaked. The group was relieved to see her senses firing.

"Of course! We got plenty," Dan chuckled, and Emily came back to life as she ate, while Trevor and Gwen munched on a couple of orange berries as well. Dan, pleased with the situation, sat on the ground.

"What's our next move?" Trevor asked Dan as they ate. Dan shrugged, wishing he had a concrete answer for him.

"We wait and we hope, Trevor."

CHAPTER 6: Emergency Measures

George shut the communicator down. Annie and Peter got up from their chairs, looking at him expectantly. George shook his head, and they both slumped back into their swivel chairs. It was a cold, rainy afternoon, and The Factory was practically deserted except for George, Annie and Peter. They sat in The Factory's newest installment, deemed the Bright Room by Marv at its opening. The room was expansive, almost twice as big as many of the dorms, but it was also extremely empty, with only a large round table filling up the furniture space. Each wall was almost completely covered with a window, letting light shine in intensely on most days, hence Marv's name choice.

However, on this day it was as gloomy as it had ever been. This room was created to birth wonderful and life-changing inventions and ideas; magnificent additions to their books, among other magical things, but this day there was none of that, only sorrow, worry, and stress.

"George, what are we going to do? It's been much too long for them to go without contacting us. Something simply must've happened!" Annie cried, her forehead creased like origami, but George remained silent, stroking his beard as he paced around the front of the room next to the main window. Peter nodded and chimed in,

"Professor, Annie's right. This isn't normal, they woulda picked up our call with the communicator--"

"I'm well aware of that, Peter," George cut him off sharply. Silence filled the spacious room. George propped himself up against the table and put both hands on his head. The situation was undeniably sticky. Peter and Annie looked at each other, unsure of what to do. Suddenly, Peter sat up.

"Professor George, I'll go to Brazil. I'll find Kris. You two need to save the others. I know they're in trouble." Annie looked at Peter. In her face, Peter could see all kinds of protest and disagreement brewing in her mind. Before she could say any of it, Peter pushed his chair as close to hers as he could get it, and placed both his hands on her cheeks. Peter locked eyes with her.

"You know it's the right thing to do," he said softly, trying to comfort her. She slowly nodded, but was obviously distressed. Peter pulled her in and kissed her, and Annie embraced him tightly. George hadn't spoken yet.

"Peter, how are we going to find them? Their signal doesn't show up on our radar!" Annie asked once they pulled apart, still slightly hoping Peter would rescind his plan. Then, a noise.

"Hmmph. Peter's right, we need to find them," George chimed in, rubbing his hands together.

"Well answer my question, how are we to know where Dan and the others are?" Annie asked again, this time to George. None of them spoke for a while. Peter put his head down on the table, and Annie scrunched up her face, as George seemed to be deep in his own thoughts.

"Let's do some research. There's not much else we can do, right?" Annie suggested. George went into the corridor to grab a couple of laptops. They each sat by the table and opened a computer.

"I'll pull up the history of their coordinates before the signal shut off," Peter said. He typed in a couple of commands, and on his screen popped up a line of blue dots, before a sudden stop. Annie pointed at the place where the blue dots ceased to appear.

"Zoom in here," she said. Peter did so, bringing the screen up to 500%. There was an extremely fine line going across the map right where the dots stopped. It read, *Lagoon Line - previously*.

THE LOST JEWEL

"Why previously?" Annie questioned. George quickly opened a search browser on his own laptop and slapped his screen in triumph.

"Here you go, Annie," He exclaimed, and the screen read:

Lagoon Line:
This geographical location has been thoroughly researched over the past hundred years since rumors began to sprout from media that a plane going from Italy to Argentina crashed and its pattern showed a complete disappearance at these coordinates.

Since its conception, this line has been deemed as the general area which an island named Lagoon Island is - a place where the aforementioned plane may have crashed on, with traits similar to the Bermuda Triangle. However, since scientists Richard Lagoon and Sarah Silvo first released their thesis on the possibility of this landform, they've come forward with a conclusion that this island most likely does not exist, and therefore, this line was removed from maps around the world, and is only kept in certain advanced technological applications as a point of reference.

"Sarah Silvo and Richard Lagoon... Who are they? George?" Peter asked, looking over at the professor. He had a large grin on his face.

"We went to Dartmouth together. Sarah, I mean. I can contact her. We can get information about this. We can find them!" George practically shouted. Annie and Peter looked at each other and couldn't help but smile. Then, Peter got up and pushed his chair in, walked over to Annie and put his hand on her shoulder.

"You guys can go after them. I need to go to Brazil." Annie wanted to protest, but Peter gripped her shoulder tightly, which to Annie felt like a plea to understand, so she sat quietly.

"That can be arranged. A man as intelligent as I has a deep breadth of connections," George winked, laughing as Peter and Annie gagged in unison.

"Hold on a moment," George waved them off as he pulled out his cell phone. Annie and Peter slowly walked out of the Bright Room. Peter reached over and grabbed her hand, holding it softly. Once they were out of George's sight, Annie placed her hand on Peter's chest, and he stopped walking. Annie looked up into his eyes, and gulped, holding back tears.

"When will I see you again?" Peter's face showcased a strained smile as he ran his fingers through her thin, blonde hair. A single tear fell from her eye and he caught it before it rolled all the way down.

"Annie, you and I won't ever be apart. I'll see you before you know it," he assured her, and kissed her cheek

THE LOST JEWEL

lovingly. Annie pulled him in close and hugged him, squeezing to the point where Peter pretended to gasp for air.

"Hey! Get back in here, lovebirds!" Peter and Annie scurried back into the room, and George tossed a ticket towards Peter. He looked down to read it, and immediately realized it was a plane ticket.

"George, you're a magician!" He exclaimed, and George attempted to remain modest.

"Annie, we have one too. Unfortunately magic can't change departure times. See you two bright and early tomorrow morning!" George happily walked out of the room, whistling an upbeat tone as he shut the door behind him. Annie and Peter looked at their tickets to find the departure time. It read, *Estimated DEPT: 4:00AM.*

They glanced at each other, and slumped back into their chairs one more time, completely defeated.

A gigantic screen, spanning the entirety of one wall in front of everyone in the room, buzzed and whirred for five minutes before an image finally clearly appeared. Justin sat before the screen, eyes a piercing green and hair blonde and long. His cloak was large; a dark suede blue. The picture seemed to be frozen, however.

"Sir? Moop, did you mess this transmission up? What the heck did you do?" King Zala said, glaring at his tiny servant. Moop jumped out of his seat, trembling in fear.

THE LOST JEWEL

"Oh, heavens no, sir, I would never, I-I promise I didn't touch the screen!" Moop stammered, blubbering like a baby.

"Silence!" Justin's voice ran through the room and caught the attention of King Zala, Moop, and Bailey. They all shut their mouths and paid attention to the screen. The picture had correctly loaded on Justin's side, so he began.

"You, Zala, have done a less than exemplary job," Justin began, staring directly at King Zala, who tried avoiding eye contact by looking down at his shoes. Tanner walked into sight on the screen, hands full with papers.

"Thanks to me, though, your sloppy work has actually gained us some leverage in this case!" Tanner smirked. King Zala perked up, raising a bushy eyebrow at Tanner.

"How do you mean?" Bailey, who had been in the room the whole time but hadn't spoken until now, asked.

"It's simple," Tanner replied. "Read this!" He stuck a paper out in front of the camera so that the words would be legible for King Zala, Bailey and Moop. It was a licensing deal for an invention by TJ, Tanner and Justin's corporation. The picture on the paper was a bright blue orb with a glowing yellow aurora around it, and in the picture it was placed on a young man's belt. The words were technical and much too complicated for Zala make sense of, but Tanner explained what King Zala couldn't understand.

THE LOST JEWEL

"Your soldiers may have been too stupid to keep Kris contained, but one of them did accidentally place one of my masterful inventions in his bag!" King Zala understood this as a victory and let out a whoop of delight, but Bailey remained complacent. He pointed at the depiction of the orb's picture.

"Tanner, wouldn't Kris easily be able to find an orb like that on his sack?" Tanner scoffed at the question as if it was preposterous.

"I'm not daft. When the orb is placed on a target, it shrinks to a microscopic size, invisible to the naked eye," he explained. Moop was mesmerized by the contraption, staring deeply at the photo.

"C-Can I have one?" He mumbled, eyes wide. King Zala turned to his servant and screamed at the top of his lungs,

"Moop, don't you dare speak again or I'll kill you and Bailey and eat the both of you for supper!" Moop shuddered and bowed in the direction of King Zala, slowly inching away as he did so.

"Anyway…" Justin tried to get back the room, and King Zala turned his attention back to the screen.

"With this device we'll be able to find Kris and his travel companions with ease, and the jewel will be ours. All we need is for your soldiers to follow the directions we send to you, Zala," Justin said. King Zala nodded, and the transmission was promptly ended, leaving nothing in the room but a low humming noise from the screen.

"Moop, attend to Vajra. Bailey, organize the troops and head the hunt for Kris. Alissa will be here soon, and more importantly, the jewel!" He cackled. Moop and Bailey ran off to their assignments quickly.

Moop went down the staircase carefully, as his small frame gave him a vulnerability to falls and other issues that would be minor to other people. Vajra heard Moops footsteps coming down the spiraling staircase. The area Vajra was being held in had a putrid smell to it, as bad as a New York sewer, and the stairs were covered with cobwebs and dead moss, among other bugs and dirt. The walls were peeling and everywhere looked dreary, but Vajra had tried his best to remain sane in the rotten place. Once Moop reached the final step, he waved at Vajra, flashing a smile.

"Hey, Vajra! Vaj-daddy. Vajio!" He pointed his fingers at Vajra excitedly, without a response from the prisoner. After a minute, Moop shrugged and disappeared to the kitchen to fix a meal for Vajra. As he opened the fridge, Vajra noticed that this time around, Moop had a key looped around his belt. *This is intriguing,* Vajra thought to himself.

"Hey Moop?" He started. Moop was busy scrubbing dishes, but looked over at Vajra.

"Do you like King Zala?" This question caused Moop to pause what he was doing. He set the plate down in the sink and sighed under his breath, looking down at his feet. He scratched his hair with his free hand.

"I mean, he treats you pretty badly. It seems unfair to me. I just don't know why you put up with it." Vajra pressed on. Moop stared harder at the ground, resisting any urge to look up and into Vajra's eyes. He tried to fight it, but thoughts began to enter Moop's mind - thoughts of King Zala bellowing orders, threatening to kill Moop, blowing him off as if he were only a speck in Zala's monstrous reign.

"Moop... You don't have to take this. Use your key, let me out, and we'll find Alissa before King Zala does. We'll stop him in his tracks. That'll teach him to mess with you again!" Vajra urged. Moop was motionless. Vajra waited impatiently for something, anything to signify that Moop was on board. He'd never witnessed Moop stay silent for this long. Finally, Moop pulled off his yellow rubber glove and dropped the sponge he was using. He made his way over to Vajra's cell and unlocked it, saying nothing as he did so. He then promptly jumped into Vajra's arms, not missing a beat.

"Thank you," he cried, "thank you for setting me free!" Vajra, relieved that his plan had worked, nodded and smiled.

"Any time, Moop. Now let's go, time is not something we should be wasting right now," he said, setting Moop back on the ground. Moop led the way, stopping Vajra at the top of the stairs in order for him to make sure no one was coming through the corridor. They quickly dashed through the palace, hiding behind corners when people came into view. Finally, they reached the back door, which Moop opened with his keys.

"Now what?" Moop asked, and Vajra pointed to the entrance of the jungle. Without another word, the two jogged in that direction, leaving the village behind.

CHAPTER 7: Giving Insight

"It's nice to see you again, Juniper." Sarah Silvo's house was quaint and had a faint smell of rosemary, which fit her personality quite well. The walls were covered with a quirky mix of framed, professionally taken dog photos and Dartmouth memorabilia. The living room where Annie and George sat was large, with a TV in the center and an awkwardly shaped white couch in front of the screen. It was an odd setup, complete with randomly placed lamps and candles lining the corners and outsides of the rooms. To top it all off, Sarah sat calmly on a stack of four pillows with her legs crossed tightly underneath her, as if she were meditating.

"So, what brings you here?" She asked. George sighed, and Annie shuffled her feet.

"Sarah, we're interested in learning more about your research on Lagoon Line and the Island," George explained, taking care to say everything nicely. He knew how it was to talk about a theory that had been ripped down by media as a scientist. Sarah gave them a pained smile and got up, motioning for them to follow her.

The library that Sarah led George and Annie to was just as unorthodox as the living room, with bookshelves bolted to the ground instead of the walls. Annie was perplexed by the oddities of the room, but George focused on Sarah. She pulled out a novel from one of the shelves and opened it to a certain page that was previously bookmarked.

"If you look here, you'll see where I theorized the Lagoon Island could be, based on the solstices of course," Sarah explained as George examined the page. Annie stood behind him, awkwardly twiddling her fingers.

"And if you had to guess, where do you think it would be now?" George implored. Sarah pulled a pen out from the labcoat she was wearing and scribbled a mess of calculations on the page, occasionally pausing to shut her eyes tightly for a moment before going back to her work. Finally, she gave George and Annie her prediction.

"If my calculations are correct, these are the coordinates of the island," Sarah wrote the numbers down on a page in the book and ripped it out, handing it to George.

"Thank you very much, Sarah. I'd love to stay longer and catch up, but we're in a rush, so…" George trailed off, but Sarah only laughed.

"Oh, of course! Let me know if you find the dang thing. Maybe I'll get some credibility back," she joked, but Annie had a feeling that she might be serious. As they walked back to their car, Annie poked George's shoulder.

"So how are we gonna get from Hanover to Lagoon Island? Doubt there are any direct flights," she chuckled lightly, but George had a stern expression on his face. He opened the door to the car, revved up the engine, and they sped off down the road.

THE LOST JEWEL

"I have a couple of fellow grads that work down by a dock that can get us there. Just be patient, Annie," George said, and Annie complied with his wishes. She was restless, however. She knew wherever Dan and the others were, they were in danger, and the longer she and George took, the worse their chances were.

Peter woke up groggily, rubbing his eyes and yawning. He checked his watch, and the time shocked him. He shot up from his seat, slamming his head on the top of the plane. He cursed, massaging the damaged area. A little static came from the speakers, and then a voice.

"Thank you for flying with us. We have arrived in Brazil. Please exit the plane in an orderly manner." Peter grabbed his bag and rushed to the front of the plane, but before he could step off, a female flight attendant pulled him aside.

"Who are you?!" He gasped, exasperated. The lady smiled.

"I'm with George, don't worry. This is the fastest way to the jungle," She said in a hushed tone as other passengers exited. In an instant she opened a door on the side of the plane adjacent to the cockpit. Attached to the door was a long tube of which Peter couldn't see the end of. He looked back at the lady, who still had a smile on her face.

THE LOST JEWEL

"I thought we didn't even know where in Brazil Kris was. How could we know which jungle?" He asked. The lady winked.

"George took his best guess. Well, good luck!" With that, she pushed Peter into the tube, and he slid rapidly through the corridor, screaming as his body flew through for what felt like forever. Finally, after tossing and turning and being spun by the winding tube, Peter fell out the end to find himself surrounded by tall trees, their leaves creating an enormous canopy that enveloped everywhere around him. Bright and colorful foliage dotted the ground, with yellow and red shrubs and purple and blue flowers. Everywhere he looked some new creature or plant he'd never seen before was buzzing or growing. Peter had never seen anything like it. Suddenly he realized, he had no clue how to go about this search. He wasn't even sure he was in the right *jungle*. Worried, he pulled out his bag and rummaged around it, hoping George had thrown something in there to assist him. He found a couple sandwiches, some binoculars, a swimsuit, and a red glowing orb. He picked up the orb, curious as to what exactly it did. As soon as he put the orb in his palm, a yellow aurora emitted from the device, and a light blue path illuminated itself on the ground. Delighted, Peter began his trek, putting every foot exactly on the holographic path made in front of him. *Thanks, George,* Peter thought to himself, relief sweeping over him. *Maybe I can do this after all.*

Bailey dialed the two numbers and hastily threw the phone up next to his ear. The tone rang twice and then the call was picked up.

"Bailey, what is it?"

"Yeah, Tanner sir, looks like you're not the only one in this jungle that can track a blue orb."

"WHAT?!" Bailey moved the phone away from his ear in an attempt to keep it from going deaf.

"Yeah, my monitor shows that there's another orb wielder currently on the far west outskirts of the jungle slowly making their way inwards, headed straight for what our tracker says is Kris," Bailey explained, hesitant to place the phone close to his ear again. He heard a long, tired sigh come from the other end.

"Those darn Factory scientists and their copying capabilities… I'm never publishing an invention of mine in a journal again! That George character is much smarter than we anticipated…"Tanner went silent. Bailey paused.

"Sir?"

"If you're too slow to understand, I'll spell it out for you. George couldn't have known we were tracking Kris with that specific invention for sure, but with the right guess, he made it happen. Now look where we are. Fighting to beat one of his godforsaken kids in a race. Of course." Bailey waited for more.

"He even knew the exact jungle. This is ridiculous," Tanner exclaimed. Another pause. Bailey clicked a button on the phone, trying to pick up the signal again. There wasn't anything. Bailey motioned for one of his soldiers to hoist him up so he could find a way to get back in contact with Tanner. Finally, he reached a connection.

"Katie, pull up a history of all inventors we've hired in the past that are now retired," Tanner called out. Soon, he came back to the call, speaking directly to Bailey.

"Looks like someone we used to work with, Sarah Slimo or something, had a relation with George prior to her employment with us. That could have been his in," Tanner went on. "If we're going to get this jewel, we need to act fast. No hold-ups, Bailey. We're counting on you." And just like that, the signal went silent. Bailey got down from his fellow soldier's shoulders and halted the march. He positioned himself in front of all twelve troops and motioned for silence.

"Men, we have no time to waste. As of this moment, the only breaks we will be taking for the remainder of this mission will be a maximum for thirty minutes." A collective groan from the troops.

"But why, Bails?"

"Henry, it's my job to reiterate orders from the higher-ups to my troops. These were the orders. Follow them, or face the consequences," Bailey said. There wasn't a single sliver of emotion in his voice. Without another peep, the soldiers trekked on, slicing foliage as they trudged through the thick jungle.

THE LOST JEWEL

The water felt nice on Dan's sore, tired feet. He soaked them while lying on the sand, eyes closed, hands behind his head. He looked behind him and saw Emily and Trevor eating a handful of berries, laughing as Gwen chased something in the sand. Dan got up and walked towards them, curious as to what Gwen was doing. When he was close enough, he saw that she was chasing a bright red crab, about the size of Dan's feet.

"Be careful Gwen, those things can clamp down on you and hurt you," Dan instructed, but Gwen didn't seem to listen. She tried to jump onto the crab, but it scuttled out of the way in the nick of time, causing Gwen to fall flat on the sand. For good measure, the crab clamped down on her left hand, and proceeded to scuttle away.

"Yowch!" Gwen shrieked, shaking her hand rapidly. Tears began to well in her eyes, and Emily whisked her down to the shoreline to wash the wound. Trevor chuckled and sighed, shaking his head. Dan sat next to him and put his arm around Trevor.

"How are we going to get back, Dan?" Trevor said, not looking straight at Dan, but rather staring into the horizon. Dan was silent for a couple of minutes, but eventually replied, tossing some sand back and forth in front of him.

"We're just going to have to hope someone crosses by the island in a ship. I don't know, Trevor." Trevor didn't say anything, his expression decidedly pained. Dan patted his back, trying to console him.

"We can't lose hope, Trevor. That's the most important thing. You know that," Dan said, and Trevor nodded, forcing a smile. Emily and Gwen were walking back now, Gwen seemingly as good as new.

"Trevor, Dan, you guys look terrible!" Emily remarked. Dan laughed, tossing some sand Emily's way.

"We've had better days, Em," Trevor said, and Emily shrugged. Gwen seemed to be buzzing with energy, jumping up and down and zipping around Trevor and Don in circles.

"Gwen and I are going to swim for a bit, relieve some stress. Why don't you guys join us?" Emily asked, and Dan looked at Trevor. He knew from previous experience that Trevor hated swimming with a passion, and for the sake of his friend, shook his head.

"We were actually planning on taking a walk, Em. You two go ahead, we'll meet up here later," Dan explained. Emily gave him a thumbs up and led Gwen back to the water. Trevor got up and offered a hand to Dan.

"Nice quick thinking," he said, and Dan grinned.

"What can I say?" The two began to walk towards the left, kicking up sand as they did so. The scenery remained much of the same during their walk. The greenery in the jungle was almost like a green canvas splattered by a rainbow, creating a beautiful sight to behold from afar. On the other side of them, the ocean lay, calm and wondrous in its vast nature. The beach seemed to never end as the two walked.

"Hey, Dan, what's that?" Trevor pointed towards the jungle. Dan followed his finger to see an enormous mountain sticking out from the trees. It was too far away for them to tell, so the two jogged for a bit until they could make out lava slowly spilling down from the top.

"The volcano," Trevor gasped. Dan nodded, in awe as well. The geographic monstrosity towered over the two of them and made Dan incredibly nervous. The lava was far away and didn't seem to have any way of getting close enough to cause them any trouble, but Dan knew that an eruption could occur at any moment.

"This is not good," Dan said, trying to decipher what their next move should be. Trevor, in an attempt to help, said,

"Maybe it won't ever blow up, Dan." At this, Dan shook his head.

"We need to move to the other end of the island, just to be safe."

"But this is the side we landed on! This is our best chance of being found! How are we going to get Marv to the other side?" Trevor protested, but to no avail.

"It's either that, or melt at the hands of an explosion of lava," Dan's point was too logical for Trevor to dispute, and the two of them quickly traveled back to where Emily and Gwen were swimming to inform them of the news.

"A volcano?! Let's go check it out!" Gwen shouted excitedly, but Dan grabbed her and picked her up, trying to keep her from rashly running off in search of the mountain.

"There are lots of volcanos on this Earth, let's not risk our lives by getting close to this one." Dan told her. Gwen whined, but wasn't heard, as the other three had already started going the other way, and Gwen had no choice but to follow them, visibly disappointed.

About forty kilometers away from the village, the land ended and a body of water was laid out in front of the thousands of trees. An old, rusty dock was built many years ago near this border of land and sea, and that's where King Zala stood, bellowing orders to his hundreds of troops as they unloaded cargo onto the many boats that were perched nearby the old dock. Each boat was mahogany and well-constructed, with the TJ logo on the left side. Each soldier was aptly dressed in a solid black uniform with a hat to shield them from the blazing heat. King Zala turned to his side and mumbled, to no one,

"Hey, Moop, fetch me some treats from the kitchen. You can take the ride." When King Zala was met with no response, he whisked around, ready to smack his little servant into submission, but was shell-shocked to find that there wasn't a soul next to him. In all the commotion of getting ready for the boats to take off to Europe, he hadn't even noticed Moop's absence. Each soldier was marching at a constant pace, but King Zala plucked one from the crowd and held him by his shoulders, even raising him up a bit from the ground. The soldier, a younger and newly employed member of TJ's hierarchy, tried to remain calm but was extremely startled and frightened.

"Soldier, where is Moop? My servant, Moop?!" The king screamed, and the soldier shook his head.

"I have no idea, I swear, sir," the man squeaked. King Zala set him down, placing his hand on his forehead and sighing deeply.

"What's your name, kid?"

"Kyle, sir."

"Kyle. Your job for the rest of the day is to do whatever I ask of you." King Zala waited for the soldier to zip away in fear as Moop usually did. Instead, the man stood there, confused.

"Off with you, scum!" King Zala yelled, but Kyle, as scared as he was, stood firm.

"Sir... You haven't given me an order yet."

"Oh, right. Go back to the palace and fetch me some treats from the kitchen. Be snappy about it, too," King Zala chuckled at himself for being so foolish. Kyle, completely convinced that he was working for the most deranged man to ever walk this planet, simply bowed and ran off to obey his orders. King Zala perched himself at the end of the dock, watching each soldier reach the helm of their respective boat and fill it with a box of cargo. Content, King Zala smiled, licking his lips with delight. All he could think about was his chance, his one chance to erase any doubt in anyone's mind that he would rule the world someday. The king called out to the first soldier in line and summoned him to stand before him.

"What are the metrics, soldier?" King Zala asked. Without missing a beat, the soldier answered.

"Sir, we are within two days of being ready for departure." This pleased the king. He nodded and sent the soldier back off to work. Then, he pulled out from his jacket pocket an old, faded picture of his mother. She was a wiry, tired woman in her final years, with dark brown hair and thin, choppy eyebrows. Her eyes were wide and hazel to match her hair, and her mouth was permanently crooked to one side. King Zala loved her very dearly, and the picture alone almost brought him to tears,

"One day, *Ama*," he whispered, making sure not to catch the attention of any soldier. "One day, they'll all bow to me."

Lela sat on the round, fuzzy brown carpet in the living room, or what was left of it. It began to drizzle, and because of the damage, Lela had to run under the tarp her mother had placed on top of the kitchen to try to keep their rations from getting contaminated. She clung to her mother's left leg, not letting her move at all. Lela's mother chuckled, shaking her head.

"Lela, honey, you need to let go or you won't get food to eat," She soothed her, caressing Lela's hair slowly. Lela squeezed as tight as she could before letting go and climbing up the counter to sit at the top, almost eye-level with her mother.

Suddenly, the two of them heard a thunderous knock. Lela, startled, yelped and hid behind a large jar. Her mother walked over to the door and opened it to reveal a soldier standing before her. The man was drenched and his face was stained with blood.

"Come in," She said without a second thought, ushering him into the kitchen where the tarp covered the rain that was now coming down with a vengeance. Lela's mother scourged the kitchen for a clean cloth, and when she finally found one, handed it to the man. Bowing his head in grace, he washed off his body quickly with the rag.

"What ails you?" Lela's mother questioned him. Lela remained hidden behind the jar, staring at the soldier with wide eyes.

"King Zala, he... disapproved of my speed. I wasn't... I wasn't loading the boats as fast as he desired," the soldier stammered, unable to put sentences together without shuddering.

"He wasn't forgiving, ma'am... I had nowhere else to go, this was the first house I saw that wasn't completely burnt down," he tried to explain, and Lela's mother consoled him, handing him a tiny slice of bread from their rations. Lela wanted to reach out and take the bread back, but she kept perfectly still.

"Why is King Zala like this?" Lela's mother said aloud, and the soldier piped up immediately, eyes widening.

"I overheard him talking with one of his right-hand men. He told him this story, which might give some explanation…" He paused, and Lela's mother raised an eyebrow, impatient.

"Well?"

"Alright, it went like this… King Zala was a young boy in Europe, somewhere rich men took their families. His father was an extremely powerful, intelligent man - tall, strong, and feared by his peers and enemies. His wife was immaculate in every way, and the two of them were constantly busy, traveling all over the continent for their business. Because of this, Zala was mainly raised by a maid as a child. This maid, King Zala said, was named Martina.

"Martina was a calm, loving lady who did everything for Zala. Cooked meals, prepared his cloths, scheduled play dates, read him bedtime stories… Anything you can think of, Martina did. She loved Zala and wanted him to be a happy young boy, which he was. Then, one day, he woke up to the sound of screeching in the other room. He got out of his bed and tip toed towards the entrance of the room, being careful not to make himself heard. He peeked in to see Martina, cowering in fear to his father, who'd come home from a business trip overnight. In Martina's hands, Zala saw several pieces of jewelry. Zala's father smacked Martina, causing her to fall to the ground. The jewelry fell out of her hands, scattering across the floor. Zala ran back to his room. He cried all day, and his parents didn't know why - they tried to ask, but he wouldn't tell them.

"Since then, King Zala had a fiery hatred for his parents. In his eyes, Martina was the one who truly cared and loved him, and his parents simply sought to hurt her. He never forgave them, despite his parents many attempts to mend their relationship with their son. Zala sought to ruin their name and die as a ruler of all," the soldier finished the story, and Lela's mother's expression hadn't changed.

"So, basically, he's a lunatic," Lela's mother commented. The soldier chuckled and shrugged, scratching his neck.

"He seemed serious to me. I don't get it either, ma'am." The room was quiet. An hour had passed since he'd begun the story. He thanked Lela's mother many times for the hospitality and left the house. Lela's mother walked him out the door, then headed back to the kitchen.

"Come out now, baby," she called, and Lela poked her head out from behind the jar, crawling over to where Lela's mother stood. She picked Lela up and held her in her arms, pushing strands of hair behind Lela's ear.

THE LOST JEWEL

"We should get some sleep," She said quietly, and Lela yawned, snuggling up in her mother's arms. Lela's mother let herself fall onto a couch towards the front of the kitchen, one of the only furniture pieces that had made it after the fire, and in a moment, fell into a deep slumber. Lela followed suit, knocking out on top of her.

CHAPTER 8: What The Ocean Holds

Annie sat at the front of the boat, looking back at the dock that they left twenty minutes earlier. People of all kinds waved them goodbye, as if boats leaving was some sort of ritual. Most were homeless, but they all had faces of elation, like they were watching an entertaining show. Annie called to George.

"Do these people know we're not going off to war?"

"They couldn't care less. To them, it's a wonder that we're floating on water!" George cackled at his own joke, and turned back to the captain of the ship.

The captain's name was Albert Huff. George knew him from Dartmouth as well; they even lived in the same hall. Huff was a soft-spoken man with bright red hair that bopped off his head as playful curls, and his eyes were a piercing blue. His arms were bruised and heavily scratched, and the man as a whole looked like he toiled with a menacing beast every morning. George commented on this, laughing as he did so.

"Alby, my man, you look like you got beaten up this morning!" Albert grinned, shaking his head. Suddenly, his expression was more serious, and he looked right into George's eyes.

"The ocean isn't kind to those who wish to battle it day after day," he explained. George nodded as if he understood, but once Albert looked away, he glanced over at Annie and threw his hands up in confusion. Annie came closer to the two of them, making sure not to disrupt Albert's view of the ocean.

"Albert, how long until we reach the coordinates?"

"Please, call me Captain Huff. George set a bad example, but I ask of all those who board my ship to treat me with respect," the captain said this without a crack in his demeanor. A bit taken aback, Annie apologized.

"Of course, my apologies, captain." Albert paused, turning the boat slightly to get it off track of a strong current.

"To answer your question, at this rate of travel, we should reach the coordinates you gave me within the next four hours." Annie and George groaned, but Albert, almost like a machine, remained emotionless. After a good thirty minutes of almost complete silence, Captain Huff removed himself from the front of the boat, and motioned for George and Annie to follow him. They walked all the way back to the rooms under the deck, where a couple of beds lay for passengers to sleep. He invited the two of them to take a bed, and the captain himself pulled up a tall stool.

"I don't have to change course for another hour and a half, so I thought it would be a good time to take a break,"

Captain Huff remarked. Annie and George didn't know what to say, and only sat on their beds. Then, George piped up.

"So, Alby, tell us some cool stories at sea! We'd love to hear them," he encouraged. Captain Huff didn't look like he was at all interested in telling them any story, but after a second his face lightened up.

"I do have one pretty good story," he said, and Annie and George began to persuade him to tell it. Finally, the captain gave in, removing his hat and setting it down.

"Alright... A couple of years ago, I was taking a cast of characters in a play to their next show, and the trip was going to take a total of twelve hours. We left the dock late at night because one of the main characters hadn't showed up until last call. Damn actors, no respect... Finally, we left the shore, and everything was fine, until, about halfway through the trip, something snapped.

"I heard the snap from all the way at the top of the boat, on deck. Immediately, I told one of my assistants to take control of the boat while I went to check out what happened. I looked around, but there was nothing I could see. Unfortunately, there was another room I hadn't looked in yet. The lowest room in the boat, the one that controlled buoyancy among other important things, was breached. The door, normally locked, was wide open. I hurried in to see what was happening.

"What I walked into shocked me to my core..." He paused, and Annie thought he must have been doing it for effect. Then, she realized that he only paused because he had to sneeze.

"Bless you," George mumbled, so enamored in the story that he barely meant it.

"Thank you. Where was I?" Captain Huff wondered, scratching his red hair.

"The lowest room! You went in!" Annie blurted out, and Captain Huff shot her an insulted glance.

"Young lady, I'm not an elderly man yet. My memory is still in-tact. I just… needed a moment," he grumbled. Annie apologized, but mostly wanted to hear what happened next.

"So I walked in, only to see the same main character who was late, meddling with the technology! He'd fortunately only broken something minor, and we were able to complete the trip, but it was the closest I've come to not completing a trip, so I found it quite interesting," Captain Huff finished, exhaling deeply. George and Annie sat quietly, not sure what to follow up with.

"That was anticlimactic," Annie said. Suddenly, the boat rocked violently, causing Annie to slide out of the bed and fall to the ground.

"What was that?!" George shouted. Captain Huff had already ran back up to the deck, and Annie and George quickly followed him. There was only a clear sky and a calm ocean to greet them, however.

THE LOST JEWEL

"That's odd," Captain Huff said, standing completely still. Right behind him, George and Annie stood, looking around furiously for the source of the boats rocking.

"Doesn't seem like anything's happening," George commented. "Could've just been a real strong breeze."

"I've rode in the seas for twenty years, George. No breeze has ever been this strong in this type of weather." Captain Huff walked over to the hull while Annie tried to coax George back downstairs. She was worried and didn't feel like it was safe to stay on deck, but George felt like he should keep Captain Huff company. Defeated, Annie slumped down to the floor and crossed her arms. As soon as she sat down, the boat thrashed to the right this time, stronger than before, causing Annie to slide perilously close to the edge of the boat.

"Alby?!" George shouted, and Captain Huff didn't reply. It looked like he didn't know, and that made Annie feel even worse. She screamed as the boat rocked once again to the left, and a gigantic body shot out from the water, gliding over the boat and landing with a huge splash on the adjacent side of the boat.

"Impossible!" Captain Huff yelled as he tried to tie some ropes down on the other end of the deck. George was bent down next to the stairs, trying to shield himself from the onslaught of water and debris falling onto the boat.

"What is it?!" Annie yelled to him, and before the captain could reply, the beast spun out of the water yet again, this time crossing the boat diagonally. This form of acrobatics caused water to rain down on the deck, stinging Annie's eyes and flooding the ground. Materials began to float all over the place.

"It's the fabled sinner of the sea! Fellow seaman have labeled it 'Coralon'!" Captain Huff shouted, trying to get to Annie. His attempts were in vain, however, as Coralon pushed the boat backwards with its enormous fins, causing Annie's body to fly to the back of the deck, slamming against the edge.

"Why Coralon?!" Annie shouted, and Captain Huff, trying to redo the tie on the mast, called back,

"It's entire back is made up of coral, like a coral reef! That's its disguise!" He screeched back. This time, Coralon rose slowly out of the water, seemingly staring Annie right in the face. It had gigantic, menacing eyes, bright red with veiny green lines protruding out from the retina. Its skin was rough, blue and scaly, and its fin were tipped with what looked like extremely sharp feathers. It towered over the boat by a good thirty feet and from Annie's angle, she could clearly see the colorful coral reef lying on the monster's back. In a moment, it looked beautiful - with glimmering sunlight causing it to shine, the many colorful coral pieces sticking out looked like a sight to behold. However, Annie couldn't fully appreciate it as she remembered that she was on the brink of death. Coralon let out a piercing roar, blowing the boat back and causing several items to fall off the edge.

"What are we going to do?!" George yelled to no one in particular as Coralon continued to harass the ship, jumping over and rumbling under it.

"Heck if I know!" Captain Huff shouted back, this time grabbing what looked like a harpoon from a shed towards the front of the deck. He hurled it at the beast, but it missed by a sizable margin.

"It's too fast in the water!" The captain called out, but Annie had been aware of this even before he attempted to spear the beast. However, to her, it seemed like Coralon, being such a fearful monster, should have killed them and destroyed the ship by now if it truly wanted to. To her, it seemed as if the beast was toying with them purely for entertainment.

"I need to get on it," Annie realized, and George looked at her from across the deck, wide eyed.

"Annie, do you have a death wish?!" He exclaimed, but Annie was completely locked in to the task at hand. She tied a nearby rope around her waist and positioned herself on the edge of the boat the second Coralon settled in the water, allowing her to get balance before jumping. George helplessly looked at Captain Huff for support but the captained appeared to applaud Annie for her valiance.

"Good luck," he saluted her, and Annie nodded. In the next moment, Coralon spiraled out of the water, right next to where Annie was standing. Without thinking twice, Annie jumped towards it and barely caught hold of one piece of coral from the beasts' back. She screamed at the top of her lungs as the monster flung its body over the boat once more. It hadn't yet noticed that Annie was latched on. Quickly, she got her footing once the beast landed underwater. She used her legs to push forward, finally reaching Coralon's neck with enough thrusts. She grabbed it tightly and closed her eyes, preparing for the next jump. However, this time, Coralon chose to go under the boat, forcing Annie to hold her breath even longer. Her face began to turn blue as she held, squeezing for dear life as the monster contoured its body in order to rock the boat as it swam underneath. The monster rose again, which, Annie figured, meant it was preparing to roar. Annie climbed up farther as Coralon unveiled itself yet again to George and Albert. She grabbed its face and screamed in the beast's ear.

"We fear you, o' majestic Coralon, sinner of the sea! Please, spare us from your mighty strength, and we will be eternally grateful!" At first, it didn't seem to have any effect on Coralon. Annie's hopes sunk. That was her best shot. The beast seemed to be charging up its fins to smack the boat into submission. Annie closed her eyes, preparing for the worst. At the last moment, however, she felt Coralon's momentum waver. She opened her eyes, and the beast let out a monstrous screech. It lowered its head nicely and slowly, allowing Annie to balance herself on the top. It placed its head near enough to the boat for Annie to hop back on. Coralon submerged itself until it was eye level with Annie. After almost thirty seconds of simply staring at the girl, Coralon, in one swift motion, dove into the ocean and was gone. Annie let herself fall to the floor, absolutely exhausted. The emotional exertion she'd undergone was too much for her to bear, and that wasn't even considering the physical stress. George and Captain Huff sprinted to Annie's side, attempting to dry her off with the bed sheets from the room below the deck.

"Annie! Annie, say something, are you alright?!" George yelled, a great deal of fear in his voice. Annie was motionless for a moment, but finally coughed up water, and spoke.

"That sure was something," she mumbled, continuing to violently cough up water. George grinned and placed his hand on her shoulder.

"You saved our lives, Annie!" Annie gave him a weak smile, but could barely move. Captain Huff held up a hand to let George know to back off.

"She needs her rest, my friend. She got a lot taken out of her," the captain said. George nodded and got up with Captain Huff. They walked off in the other direction towards the room with the beds, and he called back to Annie,

"We'll be downstairs if you need us!" Annie acknowledged him, but remained lying down on the deck.

Thank you, Coralon, she thought to herself. She closed her eyes and drifted off.

The three of them sat around an old, run-down heat generator that Captain Huff had found in the corner of the bed room, behind a tower of boxes. Annie was still shivering and her hair was still damp, but she'd gotten some of her energy back. George and Captain Huff sat adjacent to one another, taking turns glancing at Annie and asking if she was alright.

"I'm fine, trust me!" She exclaimed, getting annoyed at the extra attention she was receiving. George and Captain Huff stopped their questioning.

"How about some tea?" She asked, and they both nodded. She got up and went over to the kettle, putting it over the busted generator. It was completely covered in dust, to the point where it wasn't even worth trying to clean.

"Captain Huff, how far away are we now?" Annie asked, pouring the hot beverage into the three cups. Captain Huff took a sip and set his cup down before acknowledging Annie.

"If that encounter with Coralon didn't push us off track, it won't be more than another hour. However, the chances of that are low. I think we've drifted east, and it'll take us at least another hour to get back on track to the island."

THE LOST JEWEL

"Well that's not so bad," George said, but Captain Huff shook his head.

"I wasn't done. This also doesn't account for the fact that our initial calculations are worth nothing now, and we'll just have to go off our intuition to get to the right spot." He paused, adjusted his cap, and continued, eyebrows furrowing as he did so.

"Due to the nature of Lagoon Island, we may not be capable of locating it." At this, Annie stamped her foot on the ground.

"We're going to find it! We have to." Annie angrily walked off to the deck, leaving Captain Huff and George alone down below. She pulled up a chair, tried to dry the seat a bit with a towel, and sat down right next to the edge of the ship. Annie looked out into the night sky, taking note of each star and their innate differences. She marveled at the calm, simple beauty of the quiet ocean at night. It had earlier terrorized her and her friends, but now lay harmless in tranquility; a complete oxymoron to its previous state.

She thought dearly of Peter. Looking into the moon, she could almost make out his face among the stars.

"Oh, Pete. I hope you're alright," She whispered. And for some reason, she believed that thousands of miles away, he heard her. She went back downstairs to find both Captain Huff and George asleep on the beds. Annie assumed this meant they still had a considerable amount of time before needing to change course, and so she curled up on to the last available bed and stared at the ceiling, thinking of her closest friends, so spread out in the world, almost all in grave danger. It wasn't hard to stay awake.

Moop and Vajra wasted no time venturing into the jungle, but after a couple of hours, their spirits had fallen a significant amount.

"Vajra… Are we there yet?" Moop whined, each step slower than the last. Vajra kept a focused demeanor, forcefully pushing leaves out of his way as he trudged through the foliage.

"No, Moop. Do you see Alissa? That answers your question." Vajra scolded, and Moop grumbled incessantly. The sun was blazing above them, but thankfully the canopy blocked almost all of the sunlight from burning the duo. However, that didn't prevent the humidity from causing both of them to sweat profusely.

"Can I have another drink?" Moop asked, tugging at Vajra's shirt. Vajra felt like he was lugging a child around, and shook his head angrily.

"Moop, we need to make this water last until we find Alissa *and* get out of this jungle," Vajra tried to explain, but once Moop realized he wasn't getting water, he had already tuned Vajra out.

Vajra, in his many years living in the village, had never dared to go this deep into the jungle. In fact, he only came close when his mother asked him to fetch some berries, and those were easy to find and didn't require him to enter the depths of the forest. As such, Vajra was extremely uncomfortable, listening closely for anything out of the ordinary. He was determined not to let something get between him and his daughter. Moop lagged behind; he wasn't used to this much walking.

"When's the next break, Vajra?" Moop said, huffing and puffing. Vajra didn't hear him, continuing on. Moop waited, and when he didn't hear a response, he shrugged and decided it must have been a silent yes. He stopped at a nearby tree and let his body slide down to the jungle floor. He wiped his forehead and took a deep breath.

"Man, this isn't easy, huh Vajra?" Again, no response.

"Vajra?" Moop looked, and realized no one was there. He jumped up.

"Vajra! Wait up!!" He screeched, sprinting in the direction he though Vajra had gone. Vajra, on the other hand, still hadn't noticed Moop was gone. He kept on walking, flicking away pesky bugs in the process.

"Thanks for calming down Moop, you were really getting on my nerves," Vajra said, still unaware of Moop's absence.

"In fact, it's really helping me see the beauty of the jungle, even though it can be quite tedious to walk through," Vajra chuckled to himself. Moop still hadn't caught up; he was sprinting as fast as he could, but his short legs could only move so quickly.

"Moop, I changed my mind. Maybe you can have some water," Vajra stopped for a second to get the canister out of his bag. At this point, Moop finally caught up to Vajra. He was positively drenched in sweat from head to toe and couldn't take a breath without wheezing. Vajra turned to look at him and gasped.

"Oh, for goodness sake! You should have told me you were in this bad shape, Moop. Here you go," Vajra, oblivious to the fact that Moop hadn't been with him for the past five minutes, held out the cannister. Moop didn't even care to question Vajra's change of heart; he snatched the container and drank.

"We're gonna have to find Alissa soon, Vajra," Moop whimpered, shaking the canister to indicate that half of the water was already gone.

"You're right," Vajra gulped. He didn't realize how his plan of escape could go to shambles before he was ever caught by King Zala's henchmen. Instead, he could starve or die of thirst.

"We have to keep going though. At this point, heading back would be a death wish," Vajra explained. Moop nodded, and they kept going. Neither spoke a word for a while, until they heard a clang.

"What was that?" Moop asked, and Vajra shrugged.

"It didn't sound like something that should be in a forest, that's for sure," he said. The two of them moved slower now, cautious of their surroundings.

"OWWW!" Moop yelled, jumping up and down. Vajra turned to him quickly.

"What? What happened?!" Vajra asked.

"I slammed my foot into something!" He answered through gritted teeth. Vajra kneeled down to get a better look at what Moop was talking about. To him, it looked like a simple, regular log with a great deal of foliage over it. After staring at it for a couple of seconds, however, Vajra realized something. He reached out and attempted to brush off some of the foliage. Like magic, the dirt and leaves on the log came off.

"This is no log," Vajra exclaimed, and Moop plopped down to see what he was talking about. The two of them teamed up to brush off all of the fake plants, in order to reveal a large, long, metal cylinder.

"What is this thing?" Moop pondered. Vajra didn't know, but he touched the cylinder, trying to think. He jumped over it and looked at the other side. In small print on the left, the cylinder read:

PROPERTY OF TJ CORPORATION - DO NOT USE WITHOUT PERMISSION FROM TJ CORPORATION

"Moop, I think this means we're on the right track," Vajra said excitedly. Moop raised an eyebrow.

"How in the world do you know that?" He asked, and Vajra pointed to the fine print. Moop squinted his eyes to read it, and grinned.

"That's the people King Zala is working for!" He exclaimed, and Vajra smiled.

"But what is this thing?" Moop asked again, motioning towards the cylinder.

"Let's follow it and see how far it goes," Vajra suggested. Without a better idea, Moop agreed and the duo followed the cylinder, dusting off the fake foliage TJ's henchmen had used to camouflage the material. It eventually led to a tall, large, out of place from the rest of the jungle. The leaves the bush was made out of had an artificial look to them. Vajra pulled Moop close and instructed him to begin pulling away the leaves of the bush. With the duo's combined effort, they wasted no time in uncovering the cylinder's end - the head of a snake, larger than Vajra's home back in the village. It was brown like the rest of the contraption, but its eyes seemed to be transparent. Moop began to take a step towards it but Vajra stopped him.

"Let's make sure we're alone first," Vajra said. The two of them scoped the area, and they couldn't find a single soul, so the two of them entered the clearing. As they came closer to the snake head, they could see that its eyes were transparent because they were windows.

"That looks like some sort of control room," Vajra guessed. Moop kicked the side of the head, startled to hear the loud crackle that erupted from the mechanical beast.

"Be careful," Vajra hissed. Moop hurriedly went back to Vajra's side, promising that he wouldn't step out of line again. With great care, Vajra made his way to the very front of the snake head, and spent a couple of minutes trying to figure out how to get into the room that was inside. Eventually, he found a door, where the snake's chin would be, but it was locked. A key pad was next to the door handle.

"Seems like there's a key code," he explained to Moop.

"Let's get out of here. I'm sure Zala's people will be coming to this area at some point, and we don't want to be there when that happens," Vajra instructed. They quietly walked out of the clearing together. Once they distanced themselves from the snake, he stopped Moop for a second.

"Look, I know this is confusing for you, Moop, but you need to trust me. When Alissa is found, all will be restored in the village. Peace will reign." Moop smiled and laughed, throwing his hands forward in a gesture to brush off Vajra's serious tone.

"Vajra, come on! I know that. I trust you!"

"Good. Good. Let's continue, then," Vajra said, and that's when he heard the sound of a twig breaking nearby. Swiftly, he ushered Moop behind a tree.

"What now?" Moop trembled.

"Could be anything," Vajra said. "Maybe a jaguar." It took everything in Moop's power not to scream in fear at this. Vajra could tell.

"Hey, it's just speculation. Quiet down so we can find out for sure," Vajra whispered. The two of them slowly peeked out from behind the tree, and with the precision of a surgeon, Vajra pushed aside a bush without making a sound to see where the twig noise came from. To his surprise, there lay a young man with bleached blonde hair, a dirty, stained blue polo shirt, orange paints rolled up almost to his thighs, and a tiny orb in his left hand. He seemed to have collapsed just minutes prior and was laid out on the jungle floor, groaning.

"It's just a kid!" Moop exclaimed, and Vajra immediately told him to be quiet. He didn't want to startle the boy. They made themselves visible, but the boy's eyes were still closed.

"Hello? We come in peace." Vajra began. The boy slowly opened his eyes, sitting up. When he realized there were two humans standing before him, he gasped.

"Oh, gosh. Where am I?" He muttered, looking around. Vajra kneeled down to the boy's level.

"You're in a jungle in Brazil. It seems you may have passed out from dehydration." The boy said nothing, and seemed completely dazed.

"What's your name, son?"

"Uh, Peter."

THE LOST JEWEL

"Nice to meet you, Peter. I'm Vajra, and this is Moop. Moop, say hello."

"Hello!"

"Where are you guys from?" Peter asked, rubbing his eyes. Vajra looked at Moop, who seemed to be caught up in Peter's glistening red shoes, and then replied.

"We're from the village a few miles out. I live there, and Moop was a servant for the dictator, King Zala. At least, until he let me out of my cell and we escaped to the jungle together," Vajra explained. Peter's eyes widened.

"So you two are criminals?!" He asked, concern growing in his voice. Vajra, genuinely worried for the boy, held his hands up.

"No, my boy. I was captured because my daughter attempted to thwart the dictator's master plan. Moop was being abused by the king. We are not criminals, and we aren't going to harm you," Vajra assured, and nudged Moop, who, after a second, nodded vigorously. Peter said nothing, but appeared to calm himself a bit.

"Why are you out here? You don't look like you're from around these parts," Moop offered.

"I'm not. I'm here to find one of my friends who was captured by an evil corporation. We traced him back to here," Peter said. Vajra's ears perked up.

"Evil corporation, you say?" Peter nodded.

"Yes. He was one of my best friends. Kris, I mean. Tanner and Justin captured him, and we haven't seen or been in contact with him ever since." Vajra's eyes grew to the size of meteors and he shot up, grabbing Moop forcefully by the shoulders.

"Tanner and Justin, Moop! They're 'TJ'!" Moop tried to understand, and didn't, but nodded encouragingly to Vajra.

"Okay, but what does that tell us? We still don't know where Alissa is," Moop complained. Peter lightly tapped Vajra's shoulder, and he looked back down at the blonde boy.

"Who's Alissa?" He asked.

"That's the name of my daughter. She is presumed by the king, as well as us, to have a precious jewel that holds immense power. It's what King Zala, and, I assume Tanner and Justin, are after."

"Wow. I hadn't heard of that." Peter lay quietly for a moment, trying to think. Vajra did the same, scratching his beard mindlessly. Moop was enamored with the red orb that had previously been in Peter's hand, but had since fallen out and laid on the ground.

"What is this thing?" He asked in pure wonderment. Peter glanced over and protectively grabbed the orb.

"That's a very important item!" Peter quipped, and Moop backed away. Vajra was confused at Peter's hostility.

"Why's that, Peter?" He tried to sound as soothing and friendly as possible.

THE LOST JEWEL

"This orb is something a professor friend of mine built. Its purpose is to track my friend and show me the path to find him," Peter explained cautiously. He tightened his grip around the orb.

"In fact, that's what I was doing before I, uh, took a break. Then you two showed up." Vajra could sense Peter beginning to feel like he was in trouble, so in an effort to alleviate that, Vajra held out his bag.

"Huh?" Vajra nodded at Peter's confused expression.

"Go ahead, look through it." After a second to think it over, Peter rummaged through Vajra's bag.

"See? No weapons. No identification with TJ or anyone evil. I'm on your side, Peter." Moop chimed in,

"Me too!"

"...I believe you, I just need to be careful," Peter exhaled. "You never know."

"I respect that, son. Here, have some water," Vajra held out the canister. The boy drank, obviously grateful for the gesture. Peter got up, having finally gathered enough strength to do so, and gave Moop a friendly pat on the back.

"Well, I'm sure my friend won't want to stay locked up much longer, so I think I need to head off," Peter said, and Moop frowned.

"Why are you leaving so soon? We only just met!" Moop said. Vajra was baffled at how truly slow Moop was at times, but didn't say anything. Instead, he began to think. Knowing

Alissa, if she had come across this person Peter was looking for, she almost definitely would have helped him - she was the most caring person Vajra knew. It was a long shot, but he felt it was his best chance at finding his little girl.

"Peter!" He called out to the blonde boy, and he saw Peter stop walking and turn around.

"Yeah? Did I leave something behind?"

"No. I just thought, since you seemed to be struggling with a lack of water, us traveling as a group may help. We don't have much more than you, but it's better than nothing," Vajra tried. Peter thought this over for a moment, and seemed to agree.

"Just promise me your pal doesn't accidentally eat my orb," Peter commented. Moop had been swatting away at a bright-yellow butterfly before he heard his name was mentioned.

"What about me?!" He asked.

"We were just talking about how great you are, Moop," Vajra answered, winking at Peter. Moop's face brightened and his grin could encircle the entire earth.

"Aw, you guys! What good friends!" With that, Moop continued to chase after the butterfly. Vajra sighed, and turned to Peter.

"Lead the way, wielder of inventions," he said. Peter turned on the orb, illuminating the blue path once again, and Peter, Vajra, and Moop made their way through the jungle in pursuit of Kris and, with any luck, Alissa.

THE LOST JEWEL

THE LOST JEWEL

CHAPTER 9: Native Traditions

The sun was hotter than ever. Dan, Trevor, Emily and Dan had been walking along the beach for over six hours, and fatigue was beginning to set in. However, Dan continued to reassure the rest of the crew that they were indeed close to their destination; in other words, the opposite side of the island.

"Dan, remind me again why we need to be so far away from the volcano," Emily groaned.

"Just to be safe," Dan replied for what felt like the fiftieth time.

"My feet hurt," Gwen grumbled, viciously kicking sand up in front of her. Trevor offered to pick her up for a bit, and Gwen gladly obliged. She perched herself on top of his shoulders as they walked. Trevor now lagged behind with the added weight.

"Hey, slow down a little so I can keep up," Trevor suggested. Dan and Emily nodded. They all knew that at this point, stopping and taking a break wasn't worth their while. Their target area was within miles and Dan could see it from where they were on the beach. It was only a matter of time, or so he thought.

As they neared the other side of the island, they heard a great deal of marching.

THE LOST JEWEL

"HALT!" A voice sounded, and the group stopped in their tracks. Out of the jungle came a herd of dark skinned, short men with ridiculously long black hair and colorful paintings and markings all across their face and torsos. The only clothing these men wore were tiny skirts.

"Those residing on the other side of the island may not trespass to the Uko Tribe's side of the island," The tallest one said. Tallest didn't mean much; the tribe member stood at a meager four foot eleven. His eyes were staring straight into Dan's, as if he could see into his soul.

"We don't mean any trouble, we're just trying to get away from the volcano," Dan tried to explain. The tribe gasped.

"The volcano?! Has it spoken?" The tribe leader exclaimed, holding out the spear in his hand as a cautionary measure. Dan held his hands up, utterly startled.

"No! No no no, we were just being careful," he said. The tribe leader slowly lowered his spear. He looked at his tribe members and nodded solemnly.

"Hm. Come with us." Dan looked back at his own group of friends. They all seemed to not know what to do, and were looking at Dan for guidance. Dan shrugged and motioned for them to follow him. The tribe, almost robotically, marched in a straight line into the jungle. Dan, Emily, Trevor, and Gwen all filed in behind the last tribe member. They walked for what seemed like hours in the

THE LOST JEWEL

jungle. Gwen got Dan's attention as they continued to march.

"Dan, maybe ask one of them how close we are?" Gwen whispered. Dan shook his head. He was extremely weary of the midget warriors, they looked like they could turn hostile at any given moment.

"I'm sure we're close. Be patient," Dan said, and Gwen grumbled angrily but obliged. Finally, they stopped at a tree that was unusually large; much larger than the other trees around it. The tribe all circled around the tree, and Trevor tapped Dan on the shoulder.

"What are they doing now?" He asked, and Dan had no idea, so he simply left Trevor without a response. The tribe members began to hum some type of chant, one that sounded like a soothing melody to Dan, and they began to sway back and forth in perfect harmony. After a few moments of this, a crack formed in the tree's stump and a door began to carve its way through the wood, much to Dan's shock.

"This is some serious magic!" Emily exclaimed, and the rest of the group nodded in agreement. Once the door's outline had been completely carved out, the tribe leader left the circle and walked up to the tree stump's front side. He tapped it once with one finger, and the carving fell out, giving them an opening to walk inside the enormous tree. Each tribe member marched one by one through the carved opening mechanically. Once the last tribe member disappeared into the stump, the leader motioned for Dan and the rest to follow. Dan knelt down and squeezed himself into the door, almost unable to clear the top. Before he could catch his bearings, he realized that it wasn't a conventional hallway, but rather a slide, and he began to yell wildly as he spiraled downward, closing his eyes in fear. Once he reached the end, he plopped onto a pile of hay that was laid out nicely to break the fall. One tribe member stood at the ready next to the hay stack. He helped Dan to his feet.

"You don't want to sit there for long," The tribe member explained. In a second, Dan realized why. Gwen came crashing through the slide, slamming harshly on to the stack. Had Dan been still sitting there, he might've had to deal with a broken nose for the rest of the trip.

"Welcome to our home. You are safe from the volcano here," The tribe member said. Dan took a minute to take in his surroundings.

The interior of the hollow tree was bigger than Dan expected; etched out homes littered the walls. There was a long, winding staircase that linked every room to each other and made its way down to the bottom floor. There were several big buildings on the bottom floor; the whole thing looked like a city play set. There were shops for food, cloths, and medicine, and there were shops for people to socialize and even a theater to watch plays put on by fellow tribe members. There was a huge stage with bright red curtains, with several tribe members watching three women in funny costumes dancing.

"This is like a world on its own!" Dan said, and the tribe member nodded. The tribe leader finally came down on the slide and instead of falling on the hay stack, he bounded off right before and flipped in the air, landing perfectly in front of Dan and his friends.

"Welcome to the Uko Tree, stranger. I should formally introduce myself. I am Wuko, head of this tribe," he announced. Dan held his hand out to shake, but the tribe member instead grabbed his hand and slapped it with his own hand. Dan recoiled, pulling his hand back.

"What was that for?!" He said angrily. Wuko looked confused.

"This is how we greet people in our village. Is this not how you humans do it?" He asked. Before Dan could say anything, Emily stepped in.

"Can you show us around?" She questioned, and Wuko grinned.

"Of course! Follow me." With that, he walked towards the bustling streets ahead. Emily encouraged the rest of the group to follow suit.

As they walked, Dan was in awe at the sheer amount of tribe members, and the plethora of activities that were available. He looked in one area, and a group of tribe members were sitting around a table playing a chess game made out of bark from small tree shrubs. He looked somewhere else, and he saw three or four younger tribe members running around a playground, jumping through a wood-based obstacle course. One kid tribe member was riding an extremely tall swing, and Dan pointed it out to the tribe leader.

"Isn't that dangerous? He could fall!" Dan said worriedly. Wuko chuckled, patting Dan on the back.

"My friend, Uko tribe members are raised from birth to be the most resilient beings in this jungle. That child is just fine." Right after Wuko finished explaining, the child flew off the swing and fell roughly on the ground. However, much to the group's shock, the child didn't even shed a tear, and in fact giggled as he got up and ran back to the swing.

"What did I say? Resilient," Wuko reiterated. Dan was mystified.

"How long have you guys lived down here?" He asked Wuko as they continued the tour.

"I've been down here for a long time, my friend. More than 100 years. Though, we weren't the first tribe to inhabit the great Uko Tree," Wuko explained.

"Thousands of years ago, a man by the name of Uko woke up and found himself on the shore of this island. Dazed and confused, he got up and made his way to the forest in order to find food and survive. He had no recollection of how he got there, but he knew if he didn't find a source of food he wouldn't live long enough to remember.

"Finally, he came across this tree, and at the time it was full of juicy, delicious berries and fruits, which Uko gratefully foraged as much as possible. Eventually, his past began to come back to him. He had taken a short ferry from Brazil to a nearby island, but the ship went off course and landed here. Before Uko woke up, the ship, completely destroyed, had washed away into the ocean." Dan held up a hand, and Wuko paused.

"So, this island is close to Brazil?" Wuko sighed.

"We don't know for sure. After all, this story I'm telling you is folk lore and legend - it has never been, and never will be proven." Dan, a bit discouraged, slumped as he walked.

"Here we are," Wuko stopped in front of a small, quaint room that was only one set of stairs up from the bottom floor. He invited the four of them inside, and Gwen excitedly hurdled three stairs at a time.

"Fooood!" She exclaimed. Before Dan could say something, Wuko stopped him.

"My friend, we have plenty. You all are free to eat as much as your hearts desire."

They sat around a tiny table in Wuko's living room, with several bowls of food before them. In one, a bundle of bread rolls sat steaming, and in another, a plethora of sliced fruit and berries. Dan licked his lips and hungrily grabbed a bun, not wasting any time in stuffing it into his mouth.

"Would you like me to continue my story?" Wuko inquired. Dan nodded, mouth full of bread. Wuko smiled.

THE LOST JEWEL

"So, Uko made his life worthwhile by living near this tree, eating food from it and making daily trips to the beach in case a ship would go by and save him. However, he grew old and as the years went by, his hopes that a ship would one day come and save him were all but gone.

"So, with the strength he had left, Uko began to carve the tree out. It took an immense amount of power and energy, but with the fruit and berries offered by the tree constantly keeping him well fed, he was able to perform the task after many years.

"Once he carved enough for himself to fit in the tree, he made a makeshift home and spent his final days living inside the tree, surviving off of its immense natural power. This is when our tribe came. My great great grandfather, a very young and hopeful tribe leader at the time, had unfortunately led our population of ten valiant warriors astray from their original course and had been stranded on the island for several days.

"He came across the tree and offered their lives to Uko in exchange for guidance in how to get back to civilization. However, Uko explained that he believed there was no way back, but that this tree had kept him alive for fifty years, and he didn't plan on leaving it.

"My great great grandfather, also named Wuko, pleaded for the man to allow his tribe to live among him in the tree, and Uko agreed only if they worked for him. They agreed without a better idea in mind, and got to work the very next day.

"For years, they carved the tree out as Uko quietly watched, lying in his bed. Wuko and his tribe members were unaware that Uko was nearing his death. One day, before Wuko set out to work that morning, Uko called him over to his bed.

"What is it, my lord?" he asked. Uko calmly looked over my grandfather.

"What is your name?" Uko asked.

"I have never been given a name. From birth I was known as the tribe leader," My great grandfather responded, somewhat confused. Uko motioned for him to come closer. \

"I want you, tribe leader, to live with my name. You seem brave enough. You seem strong enough." He was taken aback at this.

"Sir, what is your name?"

"Uko. You shall now be called this."

"But, sir, I don't believe I deserve an honor such as this." Uko paused. He stroked his long, stringy beard and stared deeply at nothing in particular. Finally, he spoke.

"No. You are Wuko. The Will of Uko remains in you. Wuko." After this, Uko closed his eyes. Those were his last words.

"After Uko died, we finished hollowing out the tree, and began our life. Out of respect, we named the tree after our great predecessor, Uko." Wuko finally finished, and Dan, Emily, Trevor, and Gwen sat, completely mesmerized.

"Any questions?" Wuko said. Still, nothing.

"Are you all still hungry? Maybe I didn't put out enough food?" Wuko was confused. Dan shook his head.

"No, Wuko, we are fine. Thank you so much for the food. We're just…" He couldn't find the words.

"WOW!!" Gwen yelled. Dan grinned.

"Yes, wow. What a story." Wuko took the dishes and brought them to the kitchen, washing them as he spoke.

"Ah, well, it's what has been passed down from every Wuko before me. I agree that it is quite a wondrous tale, but one we'll unfortunately never know for sure of its truth."

"I have a question, Mr. Wuko," Gwen raised her hand like she was in class. Wuko didn't understand the gesture, but told her to go on and ask whatever she desired.

"Do you guys know how to leave the island?" Wuko took a minute to process this. Dan, worried the question might have insulted Wuko, scolded Gwen immediately. Wuko waved him off, however.

"No, the child has a good question. Unfortunately, that is one thing we haven't figured out in all our years on this island." He frowned, stacking the dishes neatly in a corner. He turned to the group, who were still sitting around the table.

"I'm not quite sure you all understand the nature of this island. It is an island of mystery, dubbed by our ancestors as the shape-shifter island. It moves, and it moves when it *wants* to move. It doesn't stay in one place, it doesn't stay in one shape. It makes sure it stays in the shadows, away from civilization, away from anything and everything." Wuko paused.

"In other words, perfect isolation." This didn't exactly excite Dan. When he looked over at his friends, they all seemed just as worried as he was. He tried to think of some way to bring their spirits up, but there wasn't much to be excited about.

"I see I've put you all in a bad mood. Please, don't fret. There is a first for everything! And while you are here, we will be happy to keep you well fed and well rested here in the Uko Tree." Dan grinned, grateful for Wuko's hospitality. Gwen raised his hand again.

"Have you guys always been this short?!"

"Gwen!!"

"Sorry, I wanted to know…"

The jungle didn't seem to end. It was the entire world, spanning millions of miles to the left, right, front and back. Everywhere she looked, Alissa saw the same thing she had seen for every day prior. She was tired of the musty, humid atmosphere that the jungle thrived in. Moreover, she was tired of being away from her family. Every night, as she lay quietly on a tree branch while Kris and Jo slept on the jungle floor, she escaped from reality to her own thoughts, diving deep into her mind. She thought about her little sister Lela, helpless without her. She saw her mother, tired and worried, wake up every day in fear, trying to keep Lela safe, but spend every waking moment thinking about Alissa. She thought about her father Vajra, who might as well be dead somewhere because of her, unable to care for her family any longer.

       She cried every night, but it wasn't a loud cry, or an obnoxious cry. It was a quiet, humble, cry, one that had one primary reason, and that was to keep her from breaking. When she cried, it didn't even wake up her companions, but cried she did, through the night, through the pitch black sky. She cried because she was scared. She wasn't sure if what she was doing was the best thing for her to do anymore. She already caused people she loved so much destruction, she didn't know if turning herself in now would be much worse. So, she cried, to keep the emotions down low. Every night, like clockwork, once she was done crying, she came to her senses, and realized that this was what she had to do. There was no answer to her family's hardship, but if she succeeded, then maybe they would be freed of that hardship. She will never find out if she gave up, however. This is why every night, after crying, she was able to go to sleep hopeful and strong.

"Alissa." She snapped out of her trance once Kris called out her name. He was hunched over and breathing heavily. Alissa jogged over, Jo already on Kris' shoulder, trying to comfort him.

"What happened, Kris?" She asked, putting her hand on his back and rubbing softly.

"I… need… food," He huffed tiredly. Alissa noticed that his face was clammy and pale, and he could barely hold his own body weight up as he stood. Alissa motioned for Jo to come with her.

"Kris, don't you worry, we'll find you some food, don't worry," She said, and in a second, she was off, running down deeper into the jungle. She didn't have to travel very far, though, because she promptly tripped over some huge plants. She screamed as she tumbled to the ground, while Jo acrobatically jumped onto a branch to avoid a fall. Angrily, Alissa glared back to see what had tripped her. To her surprise, it looked like food.

The mushrooms were large, with bright red tops and black spots littering the tops and stems. Around the mushrooms lay a plethora of mini mushrooms, like minions to their leaders. Alissa looked at Jo for confirmation, but to her shock the lemur only shrugged. It seemed as if Jo had never seen this plant before. Alissa thought it over, and quickly decided that Kris was in critical condition, and needed help immediately.

THE LOST JEWEL

"Help me grab some of these Jo," Alissa implored for his help. Between the two of them, ten mushrooms were thrown into Alissa's bag, and they hurried back to where Kris was, lying on the ground with sweat raining down his face.

"Ok Kris, we're here now, you're going to be okay. Open up," Alissa cooed, trying to sound as soothing and helpful as possible. Kris nodded and mumbled something, but he was too weak to speak coherently; what came out was gibberish. Alissa slowly opened his mouth manually and popped a mushroom in. She ate one herself, and gave one to Jo as well. Almost instantaneously, Kris sat up and color rushed back to his face.

"Wow, thank you! That was amazing!" He exclaimed. Alissa nodded and smiled. She was glad she could help Kris. Jo showed his affection as well, jumping over to Kris and wrapping his furry arms around him.

"Kris, you must have lost a lot of weight, you look smaller than I remember," Alissa commented, looking over her comrade. Kris raised an eyebrow.

"Hey, watch out, I think there's some sort of tree that's about to fall behind you," Kris pointed. Alissa turned around and saw what she thought was a tree. It was purely green and hung limply towards the right, folding over at the top. No leaves were protruding out from it, nor branches. In fact, to Alissa it almost looked like a…

THE LOST JEWEL

"Blade of grass! Kris, that's just grass!" Alissa yelled, and suddenly it hit her, why Kris looked so frail. They weren't their regular sizes anymore - they had shrunk.

"What happened?!" Kris shrieked, looking around. Alissa did as well, surveying her surroundings. Everything looked menacing now - the flowers that she once thought brought color and brightness to the jungle had gigantic pollen constantly falling off the edges, and if they got caught under one, they were sure to get squished. Small shrubs that provided fuzzy leaves to scratch one's back were dangerous, sticky traps that, if touched, would cause them to be stuck forever. Jo whimpered, obviously in fear. Alissa came very close to the other two, putting her arms around them.

"We need to find a way to get back to our normal sizes, before we get eaten," She said, trying to lead them.

"What are we gonna do?" Kris mumbled, tears falling from his chubby cheeks.

"We're going back to where I found those stupid mushrooms, and we're going to try everything to find something that'll make us big again, okay?" Alissa said, trying to sound confident. Kris nodded and he and Jo followed Alissa towards the origin spot of the magical mushrooms.

The world looked ridiculous from the angle that Alissa, Kris, and Jo saw it from. Trees were enormous giants that they couldn't even completely visibly see, as the atmosphere in their miniscule world shaded the tree's leaves from view, like mountain tops being covered by clouds. The bushes that had been normal sized previously were now like gigantic cluster of huge leaves and greenery. If they walked into one of them, Alissa was confident that they'd get lost forever. Everywhere they stepped, the trio had to be weary of blades of grass falling to the ground. Even the tiniest of flower stems could crush them at this size. Every step was calculated, and Alissa took the job of leading her two friends seriously. She took full responsibility for putting them in danger, and would not rest until she had gotten them back to their regular size. She trudged on, maneuvering around every towering blade of grass. Even the dirt looked huge to her, every single morsel of earth threatening to crush her. Suddenly, the trio heard a crunch. They all stopped dead in their tracks.

"What was that?" Kris whispered. Alissa didn't say anything. Her eyes darted from left to right trying to find the source of the sound. Jo crawled up Alissa's legs and perched onto her shoulder, hiding his body except for his head behind her. She motioned for Kris to follow her, and they dashed behind a nearby blade of grass.

"Don't make another sound," Alissa hissed. The others nodded vigorously, not interested in their lives ending anytime soon. Alissa poked her head around the corner of the blade of grass, careful not to make any more noise than what was absolutely necessary. A few yards away, several blades of grass began to rustle violently. Alissa gulped and put her hands around Kris and Jo in order to protect them. Out from the grass emerged a monstrous beast.

Its body was a sleek black that shined in the morning sun. Its head was smaller in proportion to the rest of its body, and its eyes were puny, but attached to its small head were two menacing horns that looked like a warrior's spear, deadly sharp at the end and dripping with some sort of liquid. Along with its horns it had a plethora of enormous fangs in its mouth, saliva dripping to the ground as it opened and closed, like a shark snapping its jaw.

"What the heck is it?" Kris whispered. Alissa, sweating furiously, responded.

"A stag beetle," She whispered.

"Aren't those things easily aggravated?" Kris said, and threw his hands up to his mouth once he realized he had forgotten to whisper. The stag beetle's head whipped around and focused straight on the blade of grass that the trio was hiding behind.

"Yes, yes they are," Alissa croaked, fearing that any minute the beetle would chomp down on them. She took another glance and saw that the beetle was stamping one of its legs into the ground like a bull does before charging.

"RUN!" Alissa screamed, and the trio began to sprint through the grass as the stag beetle thundered towards them, kicking up a swirl of dust in the process. Alissa could barely see with all of the debris now in the air, but she knew she couldn't stop. She continued to run, constantly looking back to make sure Kris and Jo hadn't lost her. The stag beetle, however, hadn't skipped a beat, and was right on their tail.

"Guys!" Alissa yelled back to them, jumping over a pebble in the process.

"What is it?" Kris called back.

"We're going to have to try to lose this beetle!"

"And how do you plan to do that?"

"See that tree up there?" Alissa pointed to a sturdy looking tree about forty yards ahead. Kris and Jo nodded.

"We're going to make a sharp left there and circle around the trunk. Hopefully our beetle pal won't know what hit him!" Alissa instructed. They neared the trunk, and she got ready, gaining speed. However, about ten yards away from the turn, she heard a thud. She looked back to see that Jo had accidentally ran straight into a flower stem, and was now unconscious on the ground. The stag beetle was closing in quickly. She glanced quickly between Kris and Jo.

"Kris, you go. I'll get Jo."

"But, Alissa-"

"GO!" She shouted, pointing to the tree. Without another word, he sprinted on. Alissa picked Jo up as quickly as she could and ran after Kris, now only a few steps ahead of the gargantuan beetle monster behind them. She could even feel the insect's disgusting, warm breath on her back. She could feel it closing the gap between them, and tried to run faster. She was only a couple of yards away from the tree, but she still felt that it was going to be close. The beetle was gaining speed, crashing through grass and flowers as it bulldozed its way to its prey. Alissa screamed at the top of her lungs, grabbing the edge of the tree trunk and whirling herself and Jo around like a carousel, sliding through the dirt and causing dust to fly up into the atmosphere. She continued to sprint, but after a while, stopped when she realized she had lost the beast.

"Alissa!" She heard Kris' voice close by.

"Kris, where are you?" After a little bit of searching, Alissa and Jo found Kris, hiding behind a large rock. He ran up to them and enveloped Alissa in a hug.

"Thank you…" He said between tears. Alissa grinned and patted his head lovingly.

"No problem." After a couple of seconds, Alissa pulled away, now determined.

"Let's find that antidote!" She said.

"Great, but how are we going to find it?" Kris asked. Alissa shrugged. Jo chimed in; he seemed to be trying to tell them something.

"What is it, Jo?" Alissa pondered, kneeling down to Jo's level. With his little paws, Jo motioned back and forth, one paw shaping a mushroom, and the other making an arrow to something. He moved his first paw in front of the arrow paw and made a 'poof' noise as he made his hand shimmer.

THE LOST JEWEL

"Are you saying you can find the antidote?" Alissa tried, trying to decipher what he could be saying. Happily, Jo nodded and clapped his paws together.

"Well, don't let us stop you. Lead the way!" Jo began to trot one way, using his nose to sniff around and find the correct trail to follow. After a while of walking in circles, Jo stopped and began to climb up a tree he'd been sniffing for much longer than anything else. Kris and Alissa looked at each other curiously, but neither had a better idea, so they looked for how they could follow him up the tree. Eventually, Alissa simply tried to jump up and grab the bark, but her hands missed and she slipped and fell.

"Ow!" She yelped, and Kris shook his head, refusing to follow the same fate. Jo continued to climb until he reached one of the highest branches. He looked like he was talking to the branch itself, and Jo and Alissa were shocked when the branch let down a long ladder that reached the ground. Alissa and Jo latched on and began to climb it as the branch pulled the ladder back up with Jo's help. Once the two of them reached the branch, they saw that it was not the branch, but a tiny person that had provided them with the ladder. He was about the same size as the trio was, with a long beard and disheveled black hair. His shirt was ripped in several places and his shorts were practically hanging on to his body by a thread. He had multiple scars littering his skin and his left eye was oddly blacked out and almost completely closed. Despite his shady appearance, he had a warm smile on his face and seemed genuinely pleased to see other living beings.

"Hello, welcome to my humble branch!" He said, chuckling. "I always thought that was pretty clever. How are you all?"

"Who are you?" Alissa started. The man held a tiny twig in one hand and a dagger-like weapon in his other hand, chipping away at the twig's outer cover.

"I'm Eddie, and I've been in this jungle for forty years," the man said. Alissa, Jo, and Kris all gasped.

"When I first came to Brazil, I was a shy, brainy scientist wannabe looking to learn more about the jungle's many vibrant plants and green life. However, I didn't study food enough, and couldn't find any for many days. I was on the brink of starvation when I came across those mushrooms that you all, as I can see, recently found as well.

"I was shrunk, and I had no idea what to do next. I began to teach myself how to survive in the jungle, and more importantly, how to survive at this size. It took some time, and I haven't come out of it perfectly unscathed," Eddie explained as he pulled a couple of leaves away to reveal that his left leg was missing its foot.

"Well, why didn't you ever try to find an antidote or something? That's what we're trying to do," Alissa asked. She was starting to get worried, as if this man had spent 40 years without finding a way to return to his normal size, the chances of them finding one were slim to none. Eddie smiled, and reached into his shirt. From there, he pulled out a bottle with a bright green liquid.

"The trick was burning the mushrooms over a fire and then dipping the burnt carcass in sea water. Took me eighteen years to try that method," Eddie winked at Alissa. She was awestruck.

"How do you know it works?" Kris said, obviously not convinced. Eddie pulled Kris in closer, wrapping his arm around Kris.

"You all weren't the first ones to stumble upon those mushrooms, my friends. I've helped many people that come through this place."

"Eddie!" Alissa almost yelled, and quickly apologized for interrupting.

"I have to know. If you've had the antidote for so long, why haven't you used it yourself and gone back home?" At this, Eddie frowned, crossing his arms and putting the bottle back into his shirt.

"It's not that simple, honey. I built a life for myself here. Before I shrank, I was a helpless, ignorant man who couldn't survive without the many luxuries of today's society. After the first few months, I had an epiphany of sorts. It truly disgusted me how much I relied on those things. I had to force myself to break out of that industrialized habit and become a warrior, a fighter. It changed my life. I could never go back. I've become one with the jungle." Eddie finished his monologue, breaking into a triumphant pose and grinning maniacally.

"But sir, there must be some reason why you're still here other than that!" Kris pressed on. Alissa scolded the six year old for annoying Eddie, but he didn't seem phased by the question.

"I had no family, no friends. I lived by my science, and my research. To be so integrated in the specimens that I've spent my entire career studying was an experience I knew I never wanted to leave once I got past the initial shock." Eddie explained, patting Kris on the back. Jo clapped his paws at Eddie, who nodded.

"Please, it's my pleasure," He said, handing Jo the antidote.

"What can we do to repay you?" Alissa asked. Eddie grinned hugely.

"Live to tell my story one day. When you get back." Alissa smiled and nodded gracefully. She shook his hand, and in a few moments after drinking the concoction, they were back to their regular size, falling off the branch and safely onto the ground.

Bailey finally finished carving out a sharply tended sword made from wood when his communication device began to buzz. He pulled it out of his pocket and turned it on.

"Bailey, we need updates." It was Tanner and Justin. Bailey straightened his cap quickly and cleared his throat, attempting to sound as official as possible.

"Uh, sir, what I'd like you know is that, uh, we are making great progress and will have the targets sooner than you know, sir," Bailey stammered, trying to keep his cool. Bailey, though completely fine talking to King Zala, was intimidated by Tanner and Justin. They were enigmas; nobody knew much about their backgrounds and what exactly they were after. He wasn't going to risk his own life in order to find out, though.

"Affirmative. Bailey, keep up the good work. Let the troops know their efforts are very valued up here." Tanner began to shut off the device.

"Thank you, sir," Bailey grinned proudly, and reached for the shut off button before Justin piped up.

"Oh, and Bailey?"

"Yes, sir?"

"Make sure it's sooner rather than later that you catch them. I like you, and, uh…" A pause.

"I would hate for you to disappoint us." Just like that, the communication device shut down, making an ominous final zap noise.

THE LOST JEWEL

CHAPTER 10: Rescue In Progress

Dan, Emily, Trevor, and Gwen were all out on the basketball court, passing the ball back and forth between them. Tribe members were guarding each one, but because of their lack of height, it was too easy to move the ball around and score. Dan received a bullet pass from Trevor and jumped up, flicking his wrist perfectly as the ball made a satisfying swish sound; his fourth three pointer of the game. The tribe members were getting handled by Dan and the rest of them, but were kind in their defeat. In fact, Dan thought, it was a bit unsettling.

"Great form, Dan!" One of them called, and Dan gave him a thumbs up.

"Alright, 25 to 5, right guys?" Gwen asked. She was in charge of checking the ball at the top of the key.

"DAN!" Someone shouted in the distance. Dan called for Gwen to pause the game, and met the tribe member who was running towards them halfway.

"Dan, a ship has found its way ashore!" Dan's eyes widened. He ran back to tell the rest of the group. Emily, Trevor, and Gwen all gasped, and they ran as fast as they could to the shore, barely even getting a chance to grab their things from the side of the court.

"Thank you all! For everything!" Dan yelled to the tribe as they ran. He glanced back and saw all the tribe members waving them good bye. At the front of his room stood the tribe leader, who locked eyes with Dan and winked at him.

The door to the Uko Tree swung behind them as they dashed quickly through the forest. Dan could barely contain his excitement; he had high hopes that this was the moment they were waiting for. Emily and Trevor ran beside him, but Gwen, overcome with a burst of energy, sped ahead of them, blazing a path to the beach. Before Dan, Emily, and Trevor could even get to the sand, they heard Gwen's elated screech of happiness, which all but confirmed that they had indeed been saved.

At the edge of the water and the shore stood George, Annie, and a tall, sturdy man that the group hadn't seen before. Gwen sprinted up to George and jumped into his arms, hugging him tightly. George chuckled, a tear falling down his cheek. Trevor and Emily ran over to hug Annie, all of them chatting happily. Dan walked a little slower than the rest of them, letting his friends soak it all in. He was overwhelmed with relief, and frankly hadn't completely realized that they were saved.

"Dan! Why haven't come over here?" George called to him. Dan shook his head to snap out of it and gave George a warm hug.

"Everyone, meet Captain Huff. He's the magnificent ocean connoisseur that allowed us to found this island," George announced, pointing to the tall man that stood next to them. He hadn't said a word as George and Annie rejoiced with their friends. Now, all he did was bow politely. Emily went to him and took his hand.

"Thank you. From the bottom of my heart, thank you." Captain Huff blushed and waved her off, as if it was nothing. Trevor looked around, his expression turning to one of confusion.

THE LOST JEWEL

"Hey, where's Peter?" George and Annie began to look grim. Before George could answer Trevor, Annie spoke up, getting increasingly emotional with each word.

"After we realized you all were in trouble, Peter suggested he go to Brazil and try to find Kris... That's where he is now," Annie finished, but only barely. She was obviously holding back tears. George put an arm around her, trying to comfort her.

"I wouldn't worry too much about our friend Peter," George explained to the rest of the group. "He's in good hands with my masterful inventions!" This didn't seem to assure Annie much, however. No one said anything for a while, simply trying to enjoy each other's company after having been apart for so long. After a bit, George realized something.

"Dan... Where's Marv?" George asked, looking around in search of the griffin. Dan had almost forgot. He explained what happened, and George's expression turned dark.

"Why don't we go to him now?" Dan thought about it and shrugged.

"It would take too long to walk all the way back around the island," Dan countered, "and Kris is still out there. We need to get him." At this, George grumbled but couldn't think of anything else to suggest. Then, an unlikely voice popped up.

"Since we are now on the island, it is possible for me to sail to any part of the island without losing it, as long as I stay close enough to the shore." It was Captain Huff. He spoke in a hushed, serious tone.

"We can do it then! We'll get over there in no time!" George exclaimed. Dan agreed, a little relieved they wouldn't have to leave Marv behind, and everyone quickly piled on the boat. Once the last person boarded, Captain Huff closed the deck off and within minutes, the ship began to swim swiftly through the water.

"We'll make great time at this pace!" Trevor yelled to Dan, smiling.

"George, how do you know this guy?" Dan asked. George laughed.

"How else? Dartmouth! Go Big Green!" Dan chuckled, nodding. After Kris had first been kidnapped, George spent days upon days contacting his fellow Dartmouth graduates, trying to garner information about the people that had captured one of his most loyal and valuable employees.

The water sprayed peacefully in Dan's face as they sailed, riding extremely close to the shore. After only a couple of minutes riding on the boat, they saw the griffin laid out on the shore a couple of miles away. Captain Huff increased the speed, and as they reached the griffin, he pulled the hull in order to stop the boat. George was the first, practically jumping off the ship and running at top speed toward Marv. The rest of the group followed closely behind him.

"How are you, buddy?" George asked, concern filling his voice. Marv glanced over at him and smiled.

"Oh, I'm doing fine. I'll be up and at 'em in no time." Marv coughed, obviously in a lot of pain. George looked at his trusty companion with sad, tired eyes. Dan wasn't happy either, but again felt the urgency of the moment.

"George… We don't have much time," Dan began, and Marv cut him off.

"The boy is right. You all go to Brazil. I'll be here when you all come back," Marv grunted. George took a moment, then stood up from his crouched position.

"I've decided I'm staying here. You all go without me." Everyone was in shock. Gwen shouted almost immediately in protest.

"No! I'm not leaving you again!" She bounced off the ground onto George's left leg and clung to it tightly. George smiled through the pain and gently pried Gwen off his leg.

"Marv here needs someone to gather food for him. He's obviously too weak to find food for himself now." He shrugged. "If you think about it, I wouldn't have been much help on the hunt in Brazil anyway."

"But-" Gwen started, but Trevor stopped her, holding his hand over her mouth.

"George is right. Look at Marv. We can't just leave him here. Let's go to Brazil and save Kris," Trevor said firmly. Annie, Emily, Trevor and Gwen all looked at Dan for his opinion. Dan nodded; as much as he hated to leave George, without him, Marv wouldn't last much longer.

"You guys start boarding the ship, I'll catch up," Dan said, and they obliged. Trevor carried a stubborn Gwen while Annie and Emily followed suit. George shook Captain Huff's hand.

"If it's too much trouble to sail them, Richard, I can…" George trailed off once he realized the captain wasn't willing to hear it.

"I would be happy to help. It doesn't look like there are many other options, anyway," Captain Huff remarked, and George grinned gratefully. After the captain left to get the ship ready, Dan kneeled next to Marv, who seemed to be nearing sleep.

"Marv, please stay alive. If you do, I will," Dan's voice cracked as he talked. Marv let a smile slip through the pain. Dan put his hand on Marv's wing.

"Deal?"

"It's a deal, old chap," The griffin concurred weakly. Dan gave him one last pat on the beak, and got up. He faced George, who looked as if he held the weight of the world on his shoulders.

"Keep him safe," Dan instructed.

THE LOST JEWEL

"Find our boy," George retorted. The two of them nodded in unison, and erupted in a gigantic hug. With that, Dan jogged towards the ship, trying to clear his mind so he could focus solely on how in the world he was going to save Kris.

"There's something over there!" Vajra called to Moop, who was smelling a bundle over flowers a couple of yards away. As soon as Vajra said something, Moop came running to his side.

"Who is it, Vajra?" Moop pondered, but Vajra honestly didn't know. It didn't look like a soldier, or one of Zala's undercover men. Rather, it looked like a lost little boy. The child sat near a bush, eating berries that were growing from its leaves. He had messy black hair, sharp hazel eyes, and seemed to be completely engrossed in his activity of eating his berries. In fact, Vajra thought even if he and Moop walked into the clearing, the child wouldn't notice.

"Whoever it is, he can't possibly be harmful. Look at him," Vajra commented.

"What's with all these kids running around the jungle alone?" Moop asked, then suddenly turned around, trying to figure something out. Vajra was confused, but continued to study the child.

"What is it, Moop?"

"Where'd Peter go?"

THE LOST JEWEL

The jungle seemed to get hotter as Peter spent more in more time inside of it. In fact, he wasn't sure how Moop and Vajra were still standing. He sat propped up against a tree, wiping his forehead constantly and swatting bugs away from his face. He heard a bit of commotion going on in the direction of Moop and Vajra, but didn't care to check it out. He was extremely tired, barely able to keep his eyes open. The three of them had traveled for hours, and he had insisted to Vajra that they needed a break. Thankfully, the native had agreed, so there Peter sat. However, Peter suddenly heard something near him. Out from the trees appeared a funny looking lemur, with dirty and misshapen fur and a cute, curious expression.

"Hello?" Peter said carefully, unsure what to do. The animal didn't look dangerous, but he couldn't be too careful. To Peter's surprise, shortly after the lemur came a human being - about the same age as Peter, but a girl, with long brown hair and tan skin, with stubby legs and the same type of clothing as Vajra.

"Who are you?" The girl hissed, instantly grabbing the lemur Peter assumed now to be hers.

"My name is Peter," He said carefully. He noticed how protective the girl seemed to be. Her eyebrows were heavily furrowed in stress and her body language suggested she was weary of Peter's intentions. The girl made sure she remained a respectable distance away.

"Do you work for King Zala?" The girl grunted. Peter shook his head profusely.

"No, I have no idea who that is. I'm only here to find my friend. He was kidnapped, and I had reason to believe he was somewhere in this jungle." The girl's ears perked up. She raised an eyebrow, inching closer, but only barely.

"And what's the name of this friend of yours?"

"Kris," Peter answered. The girl's eyes widened, but before she could say anything else, she heard a crash across the trees. She pointed to Peter.

"Stay right there," She instructed. Peter had no intention of moving. She ran to the source of the noise, only to find none other than…

"Papa?" She cried, unable to believe her eyes. Vajra's head shot up, and as soon as he locked eyes with the girl, he looked rejuvenated and full of life.

"Alissa!" Vajra exclaimed, and they embraced in the fullest and biggest of hugs. Moop sat awkwardly on the ground, trying to not draw attention to himself as the father and daughter moment took place.

"Never do this to me again," Vajra pleaded. Alissa nodded, tears falling quickly down her cheeks. Vajra took her hands and looked into her eyes. Alissa saw the tiredness and strain in her father's eyes.

"I promise, Papa," She hugged him tighter, meaning every word she said. Vajra pulled away for a moment.

THE LOST JEWEL

"Daughter, are the rumors true? Do you have the jewel?" Alissa nodded, patting a sack that hung near her shoulder. Vajra held her close yet again, unwilling to let go. The lemur came over and cooed curiously, nudging its head on Alissa's knee.

"Papa, this is Jo. He has been my companion in the jungle," Alissa explained. Vajra kneeled down and shook the little animals' hand.

"Thank you for keeping my daughter safe," He bowed to the lemur. Jo squeaked lovingly, and Alissa and Vajra laughed. Kris piped up.

"So, I guess this is your father?" He quipped. Alissa saw Kris and immediately remembered the blonde boy she had come across just before seeing her father. She ran back and practically dragged him over to where Kris was.

"Oh my gosh, Kris! It's you!" The blonde yelled.

"Peter!" Kris responded, and the two of them hugged.

"So this is who you were searching for?" Moop asked Peter. Smiling, Peter gave him a thumbs up. After speaking up, Alissa noticed Moop for the first time, and instinctively held her hands up to defend the rest of the group.

"Back away, Zala scum!" She shouted, but Vajra called her off.

"Alissa, Moop helped me escape. He's on our side now," He assured her. Moop nodded several times, vehemently afraid of Alissa. She put her fists down for the time being.

"Peter, can you explain *any* of this?" Kris asked.

"It seems like the man who took over Vajra's village works for the same people that kidnapped you, Kris. That would make the most sense, considering this is all happening here," Peter tried to explain. Quickly, he added, "I don't know anything for sure. Maybe George and the rest of them have found more out by now." Kris heard the name George and his face lit up.

"How's George and Gwen? What about Dan? Trevor? Emily? Are they alright?" Peter grinned.

"Yeah, they were supposed to find you, but something happened and they got lost - don't worry, though, George and Annie left to save them the same time I left for Brazil. I'm sure they have by now!" Peter finished triumphantly. Kris turned to Vajra.

"Do you know anything about why I might have been kidnapped?"

"No, unfortunately," Vajra began. "However, Alissa has a priceless jewel in her possession. This jewel, one of its kind, is worth a fortune and has immense untapped power. Moop and I know this is what King Zala was after. Maybe that has something to do with your kidnapping," he suggested.

"That could be it! It definitely explains why Kris was brought here, and it would mean that this King Zala character is part of the same organization as those thugs that took you," Peter said. Alissa nodded, and then put her hand on Vajra's shoulder.

"Papa, I did not mean to cause you any harm. I only wished to protect the village. If the jewel got in that menace Zala's hands…" Vajra comforted her, noticing that she was becoming distraught.

"My dear, no need to fret. I know that all you have is goodness in your heart. That which dissuades evil and fights for the common welfare of all on this Earth. That's how I raised you. You did what's right," He said, placing a hand on her cheek. Before they could hug again, a suspicious noise came from nearby.

"Put the reunion on hold… Sounds like we've got company," Moop whispered. The group backed into each other, looking around for the danger. In moments, a flurry of soldiers emerged from the foliage, armed with guns and swords. They completely surrounded the group, giving them no lane of escape. Out from the top of the circle came a familiar face.

"Bailey!" Moop whimpered, pointing a wobbly finger at the man who seemed to be the leader of this group of soldiers. He held up a hand, ordering the soldiers to put their weapons down. He grinned as he looked at the mix of people that stood before him. Alissa, Jo, Kris, Moop, Vajra, and Peter stood motionless in front of Bailey. He pulled out his communication device. He pressed a button.

"Send this to TJ HQ. I've hit the motherload," Bailey smirked. He let go of the recording button and turned to his troops.

"Set up camp here! John, cuff these people. Henry, alert King Zala. We'll spend the night here and by morning, our transportation to the dock will arrive." The soldiers began to get to work, pulling tents and poles out of their bags.

"You'll never get away with this!" Kris shouted. Bailey stomped over to Kris, who was immobilized by the handcuffs, until he was only an inch away from the child. Kris was revolted by the soldier's disgusting odor of old clothes and dirty socks. Bailey bent over until he was eye level with Kris. His breath smelled like the most rotten sardines to ever scourge the Earth.

"Watch me," Bailey said through gritted teeth. He chuckled quietly and maliciously as he walked away, waving for the soldiers to speed up the process. He pulled aside one soldier who had begun making the largest tent, the one they would treat as a prison for their captured group.

"Make sure you accidentally forget to feed them when the time comes," he told the soldier. The man nodded, laughing, and Bailey smiled. *Tanner and Justin will be pleased*, he thought as he surveyed the scene taking place before him. *Maybe enough for them to realize who should truly be in charge, instead of that intolerant waste of space Zala...*

CHAPTER 11: Time For Backup

King Zala sat in his room, eating grapes out of a platter held up by his replacement servant, when a soldier came running into the room, drenched in sweat.

"Sir! Sorry to interrupt," The soldier huffed, trying to catch his breath. King Zala paid him no mind, continuing to throw grapes into his gaping mouth, one by one.

"This better be good," King Zala muttered.

"You'll want to hear this, sir. Bailey has captured Alissa! And get this - Vajra and Moop were with them!" King Zala sat up. That grabbed his attention. He got up from his chair and slammed his fist down on the arm rest.

"Vajra escaped?! WITH MOOP?!" He erupted, screaming so loud the soldier thought people in Europe might've heard him. The soldier took a couple of steps back, trying to stay out of Zala's splash zone.

"Sir, it's no matter. We've captured all of them! We have the jewel!" It took several minutes for King Zala to regain his cool. He sat back down in his chair slowly.

"Do Tanner and Justin know about this?" The soldier wasn't sure. King Zala waved him off and clicked a button under the arm rest, causing a flat screen television to lower down from the ceiling. He popped the cushion off and from there pulled out a remote. He punched a combination of buttons and Tanner and Justin's headquarters popped up on the screen.

"Hello! Have you heard the news?" King Zala said, puffing his chest out as far as he could. Tanner nodded, not even looking at the screen. This annoyed Zala, who stomped his foot angrily.

"Did you not hear me? We've captured them! All of them!" King Zala shouted.

"We know," Justin countered, typing things rapidly into a computer. Neither of them seemed interested in anything Zala had to say. The king was dumbfounded.

THE LOST JEWEL

"Your first in line Bailey let us know of that hours ago. We've sent motorcycles to your palace so you can transport our prisoners to the boats." Tanner informed him, not bothering to look at the camera. Zala scratched his jaw.

"Tanner, a proposition," King Zala began. Tanner stopped what he was doing and looked at Zala impatiently.

"Send me one extra motorcycle, I want to go there myself," King Zala suggested. Tanner sighed and rolled his eyes.

"Okay. Don't screw this up, Zala," Tanner muttered. Justin leaned over near the screen and in a second, the TV was pitch black.

Dan woke up to the sound of Captain Huff shouting orders to people up on deck. Dan rose from his mattress, looking around in a dazed manner. Gwen was still asleep right next to him, and on the other mattress lay Emily and Annie. Dan didn't want to wake them, so he walked up the stairs to see Trevor hurriedly unwrapping rope as Captain Huff watched.

"Good morning," Trevor said quickly, obviously exhausted from his voice. Captain Huff noticed Dan and immediately walked over, slapping the boy's back.

"Ah, welcome! Trevor and I have been up for hours now, prepping the deck," Captain Huff said proudly. He looked back at Trevor, who was struggling to finish his task. Captain Huff looked back at Dan.

THE LOST JEWEL

"He'll make a great captain one day," Huff whispered, an immense sense of pride in his tone. Dan couldn't see it, but gave the captain a thumbs up. He walked to the edge of the deck and pointed out to the horizon.

"How close are we, Captain?" Dan asked. Captain Huff looked.

"Once Trevor's done, thirty seconds. Approximately," Captain Huff said. Dan raised an eyebrow.

"Do you mean thirty minutes?"

"Nope. Trevor!" Trevor held the last piece of rope in his hands, seemingly waiting for a signal. Captain Huff snapped his fingers, and Trevor undid the last ring. The ship instantly began to gain speed, cutting through the water like a hot knife through butter. Dan grabbed the edge tightly, trying hard not to let go.

"This'll be a great wake up call to the girls," Captain Huff called to Dan, laughing obnoxiously. Dan smiled weakly. *At least we're getting to Brazil as fast as possible,* Dan thought. Like Captain Huff promised, once thirty seconds had passed, they were right on the edge of Brazil's shore. Captain Huff pulled a map out of his coat pocket, studying the coordinates.

"Perfect," he said triumphantly, slapping the map closed. "This is it. This is the jungle!" After he said that, Dan saw Gwen, Emily and Annie ran up the stairs.

"Was there a storm?!" Annie cried. The trio's hair was incredibly frazzled from the rapid movement of the ship.

"Nope, just some sailing tricks to get you all where you need to go," Captain Huff responded. He pointed to the land, and the girls' jaws dropped.

In mere minutes, the group of kids were off the boat and on the shore. Captain Huff prepared his boat to sail, and took one last look behind him to the kids, smiling.

"I hope things go well for you all! *Bon voyage!*" Captain Huff yelled. Before Dan could yell anything back, Captain Huff released the same rope Trevor had, causing the boat to zoom into the horizon. They all waved profusely until the ship was out of sight. Dan turned to his friends, looking each one of them in the eye.

"Dan, what next? How do we find Kris?" Trevor asked him.

"Or Peter?" Annie added. Dan thought it over, walking slowly towards the jungle. It seemed to have a lot of the same traits as the jungle they'd lived in while stranded on Lagoon Island. Dan pointed to a tree that seemed to stick out from the rest.

"Gwen, climb that tree. We can scope out the area, see if we can get any clues as to where they are from an aerial view!" Gwen got to work. Quickly, the ninja spy somersaulted in the direction of the tree, scampering up its trunk as fast as a cheetah. Within seconds, the girl had climbed to the top. The rest of the group waited at the base of the tree, craning their necks up to watch Gwen.

"Anything?" Emily asked. Gwen popped her head back through the leaves.

"Smoke! I see smoke!" Gwen called.

"What direction?" Dan yelled. Gwen pointed south. Dan clapped his hands excitedly.

"We better hurry, guys. It's getting darker every second," Dan said. They all nodded. Once Gwen came down from the tree, Dan patted her head.

"Lead the way, Gwen," he instructed. She began to run in the direction of the smoke. Dan ran after her, and the rest of them filed behind him. It was a long trek, but not one of them wavered. The idea of finding their friends after so long was a fuel that would never run out. After several hours of constant jogging through the musty Brazil jungle, Gwen stopped.

"I'm pretty sure up ahead is where the smoke was coming from," She said. By then, it was almost pitch black. Thankfully, Annie had a flashlight in her pocket. She pulled it out of her bag to use, but Dan stopped her.

"No, we don't need that. It could reveal ourselves to whoever caused the smoke, and we don't know if they're friend or foe!"

"Sorry," Annie apologized, embarrassed. Dan motioned for the rest of the group to follow him. He inched closer and closer until he could make out a plethora of tents set up in a wide clearing. Each tent was small and seemed to keep a couple of men in uniform, except for one large tent that was being guarded by three men.

"Hey, look at that," Trevor, pointing to the large tent. There were several guards outside that tent, unlike the other ones.

"Looks like they're holding some people hostage in there," Dan speculated. Trevor nodded, adjusting his glasses.

"Kris could be in there!" Gwen squeaked, to which everyone immediately shushed her.

"How are we going to distract the guards?" Emily whispered. They all looked at Emily expectantly.

"What?! Me?!" She cried. Again, the group had to shush her.

"Don't give us away, Emily!" Annie said under her breath. Emily wiped sweat from her forehead.

"Alright, I'll do it. What's your plan?" She asked to no one in particular. Dan looked at the rest of them. A lightbulb went off in his mind. He put his arms around the group, as if in a football huddle.

"Okay, here's what we do. Let's dress Emily up like some native jungle-goer, have her seduce the guards to follow her, and we'll sneak in and escort everyone back out. Good? Good. Break!"

"But, but-" Emily tried to protest, but it was too late. They had already gotten to work, ripping Emily's clothes and slathering her in dirt and mud.

"Sorry," Trevor said, almost in an ashamed tone. He kissed her on the cheek, and placed a couple of leaves on her shoulder.

"You look beautiful," He commented in an attempt to lighten the situation, but Emily just grumbled. Emily walked out into the clearing after Dan gave her the okay. The guards immediately saw her and pulled out their weapons, pointing them straight at Emily. She threw her hands up.

"I'm not here for any trouble, boys," Emily pleaded.

"Why *are* you here, then?" One soldier countered, keeping his weapon on her. Emily shrugged carefully, trying her best to seem attractive. It didn't come naturally. But she tried to imagine herself attempting to impress Trevor.

"I've just been sooo lonely… I need some companionship," she said in a flirtatious tone. The guard in the middle lowered his weapon a bit. Emily gave him a wink, and he was sold. He turned to his fellow soldiers.

"Let's give this fine lady some company, then!" He suggested. The man to his left seemed to agree, but the first soldier stood firm, weapon still in position.

"Hold on, Pat. I don't trust the natives around here, they just spell trouble," the soldier said. Emily sensed his hostility and realized she had to do something drastic. She slowly pulled the straps of her shirt down below her shoulders.

"There's more where that came from. Follow me, boys," She called, turning and slowly walking into the forestry. Like clockwork, the two men stumbled towards her. The last soldier didn't seem affected by any of Emily's tactics, but followed the other two anyway, grunting in annoyance. Once a couple moments had passed, Dan motioned for the rest of the group that it was clear. They hurried into the tent, and Annie turned on the flashlight. There lay Peter, Kris, Vajra, Moop, Alissa, and Jo. Each of them woke up as Annie flashed her light on their faces. Gwen saw Kris and immediately tackled him, tears showering down her face.

"Brother! You're safe!" Gwen cried, hugging him tightly. Kris was startled, but hugged her back.

"I missed you, Gwen," He said through tears. Peter woke up and saw Dan, Emily, Trevor, and Annie staring back at him.

"You guys found us!" He yelped, and grabbed Annie, holding her and hoisting her into the air.

"Oh, Peter! Thank goodness you're okay!" Annie cried, unable to contain her excitement. Vajra got up from where he was lying and stood, shaking Dan's hand.

"I'm not sure where you have come from, but thank you," Vajra said. Dan nodded, smiling. However, he felt as if they were wasting time, and began to walk out of the tent. He turned around.

"Everyone, we can hug and kiss when we're back to safety. Let's go!" The group nodded, and everyone shuffled out quickly.

THE LOST JEWEL

Far away, the three soldiers stopped in the middle of a circle of trees. The first one, who hadn't planned to follow Emily in the first place, stopped.

"Pat, I told you not to trust these jungle people. Look at that. She's gone." The other soldiers shuffled their feet, ashamed.

"Well, maybe if we keep looking-"

"There is no more looking! We can barely see what's in front of us! Let's just head back to base." The other two soldiers sighed, looking defeated. After a short walk, the three of them resumed their post outside the tent, until the first one realized something.

"Hey, Pat…" He started.

"Yeah?"

"Why do I only hear one snore?" Immediately, the three of them ducked into the tent, only to find Moop, sleeping soundly in the corner.

"Oh no," Pat gasped. The first soldier threw up his arms. Then, they heard a rumbling outside. The three ran back outside the tent to see King Zala rolling up in a motorcycle, looking happy and a bit drunk.

"My lord!" One of the soldiers said, trembling in his boots. King Zala got off his bike, shaking the dirt off his robe.

"Where is Vajra? And Alissa?" He began. The three soldiers looked at each other and shrugged as innocently as possible. King Zala scanned the camp site, and set his eyes on the large tent.

"Move aside, boys," King Zala commanded. Unable to stop him, the three soldiers stepped out of Zala's path and immediately started backing away. King Zala opened the tent, ready to cackle victoriously, but was shocked to find only his old servant Moop in the tent. He jolted back outside and grabbed the nearest of the three soldiers by his shirt collar, hoisting him in the air.

"Where. Are. They?" King Zala grumbled, his face turning bright red with rage. The soldier could barely mumble the words out of his mouth from all of his trembling.

"They… escaped," the soldier finally said. King Zala let out a monstrous screech, heard around the world, throwing the soldier to the ground violently.

"FIND THEM!" He yelled at the top of his lungs, waking up every soldier in the site. They all began to scurry this way and that to find the lost hostages.

Meanwhile, Dan, Trevor, Annie, Gwen, Kris, Vajra, Alissa, and Jo were huddled near a particularly tall tree, one they designated to be a meeting spot with Emily after she finished the job. Dan shook Alissa's hand, introducing himself.

"Hi, I'm Dan," He started. Alissa smiled and nodded.

"I'm Alissa, and this here is Jo," She said, pointing to the furry lemur on her shoulder. Dan smiled, and turned his attention to Kris.

"Kris, are you alright?"

"For now, yeah," The boy said, grinning at Dan. "It's good to see you, Dan."

Trevor looked at Peter, who was cuddling with Annie.

"Did you figure out why Kris was captured?"

"We have no idea," Peter began, and Vajra finished his thought for him. "But we do know Kris was kidnapped by the same people who were after my Alissa. For the jewel," Vajra explained. Dan thought about it for a moment.

"Hmm... Maybe they wanted us to get distracted by kidnapping you, in order to pull off this heist," Dan offered. Peter nodded in agreement.

"According to Vajra, Alissa's jewel has power that is highly sought after. It must be in Tanner and Justin's interests," Peter exclaimed. Dan looked at the man he assumed to Vajra, who was trying to keep Alissa warm by wrapping himself behind her.

"I assume you're Vajra, sir?"

"Yes, that's right," He replied. He held out his hand for Dan to take.

"If we work together, we can make it out of this jungle alive," Dan said confidently. The man agreed. Finally,

Emily came into view, immediately wiping all the dirt and grime off her clothes.

"Well, that was an adventure," she said. They all laughed.

"Great work, Emily," Dan complimented her, and she shrugged.

"All in a day's work." Everyone laughed, and Dan rose, addressing the whole group.

"Let's get out of here."

THE LOST JEWEL

CHAPTER 12: Jungle Fever

King Zala appeared on the screen in Tanner and Justin's headquarters. Katie was the only one there to greet him, however.

"What is it, Zala?" Katie asked impatiently. Her shift was almost over, and she hadn't slept since the weekend. Tanner was supposed to take her place in ten minutes.

"Where is Tanner? And Justin?" Zala began, sounding suspicious. Katie didn't notice, as she was too tired to keep her eyes open for longer than ten seconds.

"They're asleep. Why?"

"You might want to wake them up," He started. At this, Katie laughed.

"Not on your life. Just tell me what you want to tell them, and I'll reiterate it to them when they wake up."

"Well…" King Zala paused, then took a deep breath. "They escaped." That woke Katie up quickly.

"Oh. Yeah, let me wake them up," She said, hurrying off. King Zala couldn't see what was going on, but within moments, he heard one of them scream "ARE YOU SERIOUS?" louder than he'd ever heard one of them speak. In a couple of moments, Katie appeared back on the screen.

Her face was damp and she seemed to be completely awake now.

"They're coming to Brazil," she stammered between breaths. King Zala practically jumped out of his seat.

"What? Why? I have everything under control!" Zala protested.

"They don't think so. They'll be there before sunrise," Katie finished.

"Zala, just don't ruin anything else before they arrive. Just… stay put. And, uh…" She looked genuinely frightened. Zala gulped.

"Brace yourself." After that, Katie turned off the transmitter.

Running. That's all Dan wanted to worry about. Getting away from the enemy. He had a heap of people right behind him, following him closely, even though he wasn't quite sure where he was going himself. However, he knew distancing themselves from the campsite was most important. Getting out of the jungle might take days, but it would be no use if they were captured again.

"Dan," Vajra called from the back of the line.
"Yeah?"
"Our village. Are you heading there?"
"Yeah," Dan tried not to sound like he hadn't thought of that before now.

"Once we past that large tree up ahead, I believe we're going to have to go more eastward," Vajra instructed.

THE LOST JEWEL

"Got it," Dan called. The sun had almost arrived, and that surprised Dan. He hadn't noticed how long they'd been running for. Suddenly, Dan hit something with his feet and went flying forwards.

"Dan!" Gwen cried. Dan stopped them from coming towards him.

"Don't move," Dan said. They all stopped. Dan got up slowly, looking around for what he tripped on. Vajra saw it before he did, however.

"Oh no." The old man gasped. Dan looked at Vajra.

"What? What is it?"

"The metal rod. It's something I found when I first went looking for Alissa. It's made by-" before he could finish, he was interrupted by an enormous crash as something gigantic came through the trees. The metal cylinder in front of Dan began to slide rapidly forward, and Dan scrambled to get out of the way. From out of the trees came the head of an enormous snake, but it was no regular snake; it was made of shiny, pure metal. Dan gasped, completely in shock.

"What is that thing?!" he exclaimed. Then, he made the connection. The rod was attached. It was all a trap. He looked closer into the eyes of the snake, and Dan's heart practically stopped when he saw who was sitting inside. Tanner, Justin, and Katie. The snake positioned itself high above Dan, within striking range. The rest of the group was frozen, watching the scene go on. None of them knew what to do. Dan looked over at his friends and tried to calm them down.

"Don't move," he pleaded. The group nodded, but Kris protested.

"We should help him!" He said. Emily held the child back, however. No one else spoke. They all watched with fearful eyes as the scene took place before him.

"Ahh, yes… Finally we formally meet," a voice echoed through the jungle. The snake's mouth was equipped with a speaker that emitted whatever Tanner, Justin and Katie said into a microphone in the snake's head. It looked like a control room to Dan.

"Dan 'Axel' Dames. The famous Factory worker. Valiant hero. Warrior of worlds, conqueror of monsters," Tanner announced mockingly, with Justin and Katie cackled in the background. Dan didn't move a muscle.

"What a pleasure to see you here, with all your wonderful friends." The snake whipped its tail to curl up the group near Dan.

"No!" Dan shouted, but it was too late. The group was immobilized.

"It's over, Dan," Justin came on the speaker. "We have the jewel. We have everything. You have nothing. Where are your parents to save you now?"

He's right, Dan thought to himself. *It's over. All this time, I've been fighting to save Kris, to save the world, to keep the peace, and I couldn't even do that. I'm a failure.* He laid his eyes on his group of friends, each of them with faces that told a story worth a thousand words. Dan's heart sunk. *All of these people, who love and care for me so much… I let them down. What kind of hero does that? I'm no hero. I'm nobody.* Dan closed his eyes. Then, a maniacal screech erupted from the sky.

THE LOST JEWEL

CHAPTER 13: Titans Clash, Only One Remains

Dan looked up to see an enormous plane of red flying at top speed towards them. He couldn't quite make out what it was at first, because the object was moving so fast. However, once it came close enough, he realized the identification and shrieked with joy,

"MARV!!!" The bright red griffin came crashing through the trees, spiraling itself towards the snake with an immense amount of force. On his back, George sat, bellowing a war cry and pumping his fists in the air as the beautiful bird torpedoed into the mechanical reptile. The force blew the snake back significantly, causing trees to crash onto the ground.

"It's George and Marv!" Gwen yelled happily, waving her arms wildly in the air. George looked down on the group and winked.

"Here to help!" George called.

"Look out!" Trevor shouted, but it was too late. The snake had recovered quickly and retaliated by slamming its tail in Marv's direction. George tried to pull up with the bird, but he was too slow, and the snake's monstrous tail clipped Marv's body, causing him to release a cry of pain.

"No!" Emily screamed. The griffin retreated to the sky, George still holding on. Marv coughed and coughed, and George patted his back.

THE LOST JEWEL

"Are you alright, old friend?" He started. Marv shook his head, letting several feathers fall down to earth.

"You can do it!" Dan attempted to yell so loud that anyone in the universe could hear. Marv's ears caught the frequency, and the bird smiled.

"Better than ever," Marv replied. They remained in the air, planning their next attack.

"Dang it Tanner, why didn´t you give this hunk of metal flying capabilities?" Justin grumbled. Tanner was punching buttons quickly, while Katie paced the control room.

"Where are they?" Katie asked. Neither of her companions knew. Dan watched all of this happening in awe. He had no idea what Marv and George were up to, but he hoped it would work. They were somewhere in the sky, out of sight. Annie, Emily, Trevor, Gwen, Kris, Vajra, Alissa, and Jo all had not moved since being entangled by the snakes' tail. Out of nowhere, Marv came shooting down from the sky like a meteor, with George screaming like a lunatic on his torso. Everyone watched, eyes bulging out of their face as they watched the bird and the crazy scientist risk their lives for them. Immediately upon impact with the snake, a gigantic explosion that could be heard all the way back at the village caused everyone to be blown off their feet. Everything went black.

Dan woke up to several people in police uniforms surrounding the scene. He could make out a gigantic snake head laying on the ground nearby, but the eyes of the snake were shattered. Standing right outside in handcuffs, none other than Tanner, Justin, and Katie. George walked up to Dan once he noticed that Dan was awake.

"How did you pull this off?" Dan asked. "How are you even alive?"

"Like I've always said, I'm a scientific genius. This is what I do." George winked at him. Annie woke up next, standing and wobbling this way and that.

"Oh wow, it's Sarah Silvo!" She said, pointing to the woman. George nodded.

"She called the police for us. They´re searching the land for the dictator of that nearby village, or something like that." Next, Gwen and Kris woke up. They ran to George, each one hugging one of his legs. Dan walked over to Marv, who was calmly sleeping near the tail of the snake. Gently, Dan got Marv up,

"Thanks for everything, pal," Dan said. Marv winked.

"Don´t mention it," Marv said. The rest of the group woke up, all walking to George and chatting intermittently. Vajra shook George´s hand and bowed.

"Alissa," Vajra started, and Alissa came to attention. He pointed to Kris, Gwen, and the rest of the kids.

"These are the type of people you should grow up with, my daughter. You deserve to be showered with love, with care, and with knowledge to enhance your later life." Alissa was shocked. She didn't know what to do.

"Father… what are you saying?" Vajra shed a tear as he put his hands on her shoulders and pulled her close to him.

"You don't belong in the village. Go with these magnificent people, and make a difference in the world."

THE LOST JEWEL

Alissa said nothing, but she was positively beaming.

"Before you go, you must say goodbye to your mother and Lela."

"Of course, father," Alissa bowed gratefully. She looked up at George.

"Sir--" She started, but George stopped her.

"Don´t worry about it. Someone like you, who kept one of mine one safe for so long," he pointed to Kris, "is welcome with me."

"Does anyone need a ride?" Marv called, and Vajra held Alissa´s hand as they boarded the griffin. Everyone followed suit. George climbed on last, and looked back at Tanner, Justin, and Katie, who were getting put onto a police helicopter.

"You messed with the wrong factory!" He yelled back at them, and the griffin took flight, heading straight towards the village.

Once they reached their destination, Vajra and Alissa got off. Kris began to follow, but Dan stopped him.

"Give them space," he said quietly. Kris nodded, and then looked around.

"Where´s Jo?" Upon hearing his name, the lemur popped out from under Peter´s bag to say hello. Kris, relieved, hugged the lemur tightly.

Vajra led Alissa to what used to be their home. Alissa was struck by how damaged the village truly was. Every corner of the area was burnt and scarred, completely different from the place where she had lived and grew up in. Finally they reached her old home. It was half gone, essentially. She could already feel the tears beginning to fall, but fought herself to stay firm. Vajra opened the door and called out.

"Lela! Guess who's home!" Lela came running as fast as she could. She laid her eyes on both her father and her sister, and broke down in tears. She walked up to them and hugged both with all her might, never planning to let go. Their mother came into the room, confused as to what all the ruckus was from. When she saw Vajra, however, she couldn't help but cry as well. She wrapped him in a hug, and then Alissa, too.

"Our Alissa has been helped by a spectacular group of friends, and she is going to be moving to the Americas to learn and grow and become successful." Vajra announced. "She has shown me, through her bravery and valiance in protecting the jewel and keeping our village safe from the evil King Zala, she needs to realize her true potential in the real world." Vajra kneeled down and touched Lela's nose lovingly.

"Someday, you'll follow in her footsteps." Alissa was bawling now, and wouldn't let go of her mother. She didn't know if she wanted to leave this behind.

"I'm so sorry, for everything," she muttered through tears, and her mother consoled her.

"No need to cry, my love. We want you to be happy. You did what you needed to do. It was your destiny. We are excited and hopeful for you in the next chapter of your life." Her mother looked into her eyes. "I always knew you were special, Alissa."

After a minute, Alissa nodded and let go, kissing her mother on the cheek. Then, she kneeled down to Lela's height. There was so much she felt she could say, but all she could muster was,

"I'll write you. I promise." Lela couldn't stop crying, but she seemed to understand and gave Alissa one last hug. Now, it was Vajra's turn. They embraced, and Vajra couldn't hold back the tears.

"Whatever you do, you'll make me proud."

"I love you, Papa."

"I love you too." Alissa took one last look at her family, the group of people that she loved the most. She knew deep in her heart that they wouldn't let her go if they didn't want the best for her. She walked back to the griffin slowly, looking back every couple of feet. She climbed on and smiled through the tears at her new family.

"Let's go."

King Zala, Tanner, Justin, and Katie sat in the back of the helicopter. Each person was handcuffed and unable to move. It had been an hour, and no one had said a word. Finally, King Zala mustered the courage to mention something.

"So, uh, at least it wasn't my fault!"

"Well, sir, it really was!"

"MOOP! SHUT YOUR MOUTH!" King Zala screamed at the top of his lungs. Moop was attached to King Zala's handcuffs. Tanner, Justin and Katie looked at each other and all let out a long, tired sigh.

CHAPTER 14: Finale

George invented a gargantuan generator after months of hard work, and using Alissa´s jewel as a power source, revolutionized the Factory and made it more productive than ever before. Alissa and Jo lived happily at the Factory with Dan and his parents in their section, while Trevor and Emily as well as Peter and Annie shared a hall. Gwen and Kris continued their training, becoming more advanced in their battle tactics as well as their intelligence. George watched over them with the care of a surgeon, pushing them to reach their potential, while providing them the love of a caring parent at the same time. Marv's wing never fully recovered, but he was able to fly and move through the air without an issue. Alissa was able to visit her family constantly thanks to Marv, and Vajra was happy to see her daughter thriving in a new environment. Lela was growing up quickly, and George already let Vajra knew as soon as he was ready, Lela could join them at the Factory. All was well.

"Man. We've gone through a lot, huh buddy?" Dan said. Marv moved his wing to bring Dan closer to him, and nodded.

Dan walked outside the main doors of The Factory to find Marv lying on the top of the hill, staring out the sunset. Dan sat down next to him, lying his head on Marv's wing.

"Yes. But those adventures, Dan..." Dan looked up at the griffin, with the beautiful sun setting in the background.

"Those are the kind you never forget."

ABOUT THE AUTHOR

    Aksel Taylan is from Austin, Texas. He has one twin brother and two loving parents who have supported him through everything. He loves writing, drawing, Pixar movies, and playing tennis.